Copyright 2024 by CJ Loughty

All rights reserved. No part of this pu
reproduced, distributed, or transmitted in any form or by any means, including photocopying, recording, or other electronic or mechanical methods, without the prior written permission of the publisher, except in the case of brief quotations embodied in critical reviews and certain other non-commercial uses permitted by copyright law.

This is a work of fiction. Names, characters, businesses, places, events and incidents are either the products of the author's imagination or used in a fictitious manner. Any resemblance to actual persons, living or dead, or actual events is purely coincidental.

As ever, for Suzanne & the Two Terrors ...

The Mystery at Blackhaven School

CJ Loughty

1.

History had always been Ava Greenwood's least favorite subject at school. Not because she disliked learning about the past; she would have enjoyed the lessons had it not been for the teacher, who was the problem. Mr Jones couldn't control the kids. When he told them to do something, they'd either ignore him or laugh at him. Any threats that he made about escalating things were never taken seriously. No one was ever frog-marched to the headmistress's office and nobody had ever been given a detention, as far as Ava was aware. The lesson was usually an hour of crazy frustration in which she spent most of her time clock-watching, transfixed by the steady movement of the second hand as it ticked around in circles.

At the front of the room, writing something on the whiteboard, Mr Jones was oblivious to what was happening behind him. Ruth Ribble, the school bully, was throwing paperclips at the other students. Ava saw one coming her way and ducked. The clip sailed over her head and hit the boy to her left, who then looked at her accusingly.

'It wasn't me,' she said defensively. She was careful not to draw attention to the guilty party, however.

Looking around for her next target, Ruth focused her attention on the new girl, Willow Chapman, who was sitting at the front. She'd been put there so that she was as far away from Ruth as possible. Not that it'd helped much. Ruth had been making Willow's life hell ever since Willow had started at Blackhaven School three days before.

A paperclip pinged off the side of Willow's head, but she didn't react. She just sat there, staring dead ahead, as though nothing had happened. *She knows exactly who's responsible for that*, Ava thought, *and she's figured that ignoring her is the best way to deal with things*. Ava wasn't sure whether it was or not.

The look of severe annoyance on Ruth's face suggested that it wasn't. Her best friend, Amy Blackham, who was sitting next to her, leaned in and whispered something in her ear, which brought a smile to both their faces. Ava wondered what they'd got planned and then watched in disbelief as a paperback book went flying through the air, missing its target by some distance.

The book skidded to a halt by the door, getting the attention of Mr Jones, who turned around and said, 'Who threw that? And why?' His eyes fell on Ruth and her friend. They were struggling not to laugh. 'Well, I guess that was a silly question, wasn't it? Please pick up the book, Ruth; I know it was you who threw it.'

'You do?' she retorted. 'How? Have you got eyes in the back of your head?'

This got a few sniggers of laughter from around the room.

'I don't need eyes in the back of my head,' Mr Jones answered. 'Common sense tells me that you're the guilty one here because it's always you that's the guilty one. And can you address me as sir, please? I know you don't seem to understand the concept of respect, but I think it's about time you did. You either do what I tell you to do or … we'll get the headmistress down here to see what she thinks about this.' Mr Jones puffed out his chest to show that he meant business, but he was doing a bad job of hiding the fear on his long, thin face.

Way to go, Mr Jones, Ava thought. *Finally showing some backbone!*

Ruth stayed rooted in her seat. 'That won't look good on you though, will it, sir?' she said smugly. 'Mrs Fernsby will just think that you can't control the class on your own. And is that what you're going to do every time there's some trouble in class? Call for backup because you can't handle it?' Ruth tutted her disapproval and shook her head.

Mr Jones looked as though he was faltering, as though he was giving serious thought to backing down, but then his expression hardened and he once again stuck out his chest. 'I don't *care* if it makes me look weak in front of the headmistress. If that's what it takes to get you to alter your attitude, then I'm prepared to live with that. I'll ask you one last time to pick up the book and then we begin escalating this silly little situation.'

Now it was Ruth's turn to look uncertain about what to do. For a second it looked as if she would stay put and take her chances. But then she stood up and marched angrily to the front of the class. As she scooped up the book and returned to her seat, she dished out a dirty look. Not toward the teacher, though – not towards Mr Jones. The dirty look was directed at Willow – the new girl – as if Ruth somehow blamed her for what'd happened.

The rest of the lesson passed by without any further incidents of bad behavior.

2.

At break time, in the playground, Ava told her best friend, Libby, about everything that had happened.

'Ah, man, I wish I'd been there to see that,' Libby said, giving her long, straight, blonde hair a flick over her shoulder. 'Mr Jones has finally managed to man up and grow a spine. I almost need to have seen it with my own eyes to believe it.'

'You should have seen the look on Ruth's face. I wish I could have got a picture.'

'She'll have it in for him. She won't let *that* slide.'

'Like most bullies, she likes to target the weak, so I don't think she'll give him as much trouble now. Not if he continues to stand up to her.'

'Let's hope he does.'

Ava explained about the dirty look that Ruth had given the new girl as she'd gone to retrieve the book. 'She's definitely not done with her,' she said. 'Ruth will take her frustrations out on her. Unless she can grow a spine like Mr Jones has and stick up for herself.'

'I guess we'll have to wait and see.'

Ava looked over her friend's shoulder, toward the other side of the playground. 'Well, I don't think we're going to have to wait long,' she said, pointing, 'because it looks like things are about to kick off over there, look.'

Ruth and Amy were making their way over to Willow, who didn't notice them until it was too late. She looked shocked as they appeared in front of her.

Ava and Libby moved closer so they could hear what was being said.

'You nearly got me in trouble with the headmistress earlier,' Ruth said to Willow.

'How?' Willow replied, staring at her in disbelief.

'I was trying to get your attention in class and you blanked me,' Ruth explained. '*That's* why I threw that book at you. You knew perfectly well that I wanted you to turn around and look at me.'

'Yeah, you knew perfectly well,' Amy said, jabbing Willow with her finger.

Willow put herself up on her tiptoes and began looking around.

'I can't see any teachers around,' Ava said to Libby, 'which is probably what she's looking for.'

'Please just leave me alone,' Willow said. She attempted to flee but Amy moved to block her way. 'I haven't done anything to you, so why are you targeting me?'

'We're not targeting you,' Amy said, 'we just want to talk.'

'Yeah, we just want to talk,' Ruth said, taking a step closer to Willow, who was once again looking around frantically on her tiptoes. 'You never answered my question. Why did you ignore me in class when I was trying to get your attention? Oh, and where did you get your uniform? From a jumble sale? Is that a second-hand jumper, because it doesn't look new?'

Tears were beginning to form in Willow's eyes and her bottom lip was quivering. She opened her mouth to say something but then darted to her left in an attempt to get away. For a second it looked as if she might do it, but then a slab of a hand grabbed her by the shoulder and yanked her back.

'You're not doing yourself any favors here, you know,' Ruth said, giving Willow a hard shove. She struggled to stay on her feet as she was sent reeling.

And then a loud, booming voice echoed across the playground, startling everyone. Ruth and Amy began scurrying away in an attempt to distance themselves from the situation. And everyone nearby stopped what they were doing to watch the drama unfold ...

'Eh, where are you going!' Mrs Fernsby, the headmistress, said, halting the girls in their tracks. 'Well, well, well, there's some trouble and you pair are involved. Who would have thought it! Come on then, give me some wishy-washy excuse for what I just witnessed?' she said, leveling the question at Ruth. 'Don't tell me, you were just playing around and didn't mean to shove the new girl hard enough to nearly knock her over, right?'

'Err, yeah ... that's exactly what we were doing,' Ruth said.

Mrs Fernsby rolled her eyes and said, 'Ever since you came to this school two months ago you've been nothing but trouble. Why are you so hell-bent on making some kids' lives hell? Just what exactly is your problem?' She waited a few seconds for an answer, then shook her head. 'You had a detention last week. That doesn't appear to have done the trick, does it? So how about another one? Or maybe two? Would *that* have any effect on your attitude?'

Ruth's jaw dropped. '*What!*' she said, aghast. 'No way! That'd be *so* unfair!'

'Would it?' Mrs Fernsby said. 'Would it really be unfair?' She didn't wait for a reply. 'Okay, here's where we're at. If I see or hear about you causing any problems at this school, I'm going to make sure that you are well punished. Is any of this registering with you? Do we have an understanding?'

Ruth opened her mouth to protest. 'But ...'

'No buts,' Mrs Fernsby said, dismissing her with quick flicks of her fingers. 'Just get out of my sight and think long and hard about which direction you're taking in life, little miss, because you're heading down the wrong path, I can assure you.'

Looking both sullen and angry at the same time, Ruth began moving away with Amy just as the bell sounded to end break time.

Mrs Fernsby clapped her hands together and beckoned all the onlookers to get moving as well. And then she went to Willow to see if she was okay.

'She looks really upset,' Ava said as she and Libby walked toward the main entrance. 'I feel sorry for her because she hasn't got any friends yet. D'you think we should hang out with her? Perhaps invite her to the park after school or something? She'll probably be quite cool if we can get her talking.'

'I'm not sure being friends with her would be such a good idea at the moment,' Libby responded, shaking her head. 'Ruth will be targeting her and anyone around her will be in the line of fire. That's some stress that I don't need in my life. That's *avoidable* stress. We already have enough problems with Ruth and Amy without adding fuel to the fire.'

'Yeah, I suppose you've got a point,' Ava had to admit.

But she still felt as if she needed to do something to let the new girl know that there was at least one friendly face at the school. With that in mind, just before she disappeared inside the building, Ava to tried catch Willow's eye so she could offer her a smile. It was no good, however, because Willow was still too busy talking to the headmistress to notice anyone else.

3.

The next flare-up of trouble came in the dinner hall. Willow was sitting at the back of the room, in a corner. Hunched over her tray, she was scanning through the pages of a thick book while picking at her food, taking the occasional mouthful. Ava wasn't surprised to see that she was on her own.

She and Libby were in the queue to get their food, making their selections as they progressed. Libby opted for mash, chicken pie and peas, soaked with thick gravy. And Ava plumped for the same, but with chips instead of mash. After they'd got their drinks, they stood together for a minute, making the important decision of where to sit.

Libby followed her friend's gaze and said. 'Err, no, I know what you're going to suggest and that would not be a good idea.'

'I feel sorry for her,' Ava said, looking at the new girl. 'You wouldn't like it if you were at a new school and had no friends. You wouldn't like it if you were the only one sat on your own while everyone else was huddled in groups, chatting and having a laugh, would you?'

'No, of course not, but ...' Libby glanced around the room, scanning the whole area.

'She's not here and neither is her sidekick,' Ava said. 'I've already checked. They've probably snuck out to go to the chip shop. They like doing that on Wednesdays, I've noticed.'

'What if they haven't snuck out?' Libby said. 'What if they're just late getting to the hall? If they see us talking to her ...'

Appearing to have tuned out to what her friend was now saying, Ava began making her way across the room. When she realized that Libby wasn't with her, she turned and beckoned her to follow. For a few seconds Libby stood rooted to the spot, shaking her head – then she rolled her eyes and scurried to catch up.

'This is a bad, *bad* idea,' Libby said in Ava's ear as she moved alongside her. 'I think we should back out of this. I *really* don't want this to be one of those "I told you so" moments.'

But once again, Ava appeared to be tuned out to what her friend was suggesting.

As they neared the table where Willow was sitting, she caught sight of them bearing down on her and hurriedly packed the book away in her bag.

'Hi,' Ava said, smiling, wanting to appear as amiable as possible, 'is it okay if we sit with you?'

She didn't wait for a reply. She just plonked herself down opposite Willow and continued to smile.

Libby offered a more apologetic expression as she slid in next to Ava.

'Ah, you opted for the pie as well,' Ava said in an attempt to break the ice. 'Great minds think alike and all that.'

Willow said nothing in reply; she just looked from one girl to the other, clearly not comfortable with the situation she now found herself in.

'I'm sorry about my friend,' Libby said, 'she can be a little embarrassing at times, but she just thought it would be nice if we came over to introduce ourselves to you, what with you being new at the school and all.'

'Hey, who are you calling embarrassing?' Ava said, playfully elbowing her friend on the arm. 'I won't apologize for being friendly. If I was a new student here I'd want someone to talk to me. So that's why we're here.' She splayed her hands and did a ta-da! gesture. 'To try and make you feel welcome, especially after everything that's happened with Ruth so far. I wouldn't worry too much about her. It's nothing personal. If it wasn't you, it'd be someone else. She's got mental health issues, that girl. I'd steer well clear of her if I was you.'

'I think she already knows to do that,' Libby said.

An awkward silence followed, in which all three girls kept looking at each other, not knowing what to say next.

And then Libby spotted an unwelcome sight on the other side of the room. 'Look who just joined the queue,' she said, nodding. 'Now might be a good time to move to another table,' she whispered in Ava's ear, 'before we get noticed.'

Ava briefly considered her friend's suggestion but then decided to stay put. 'I don't think she'll risk getting in any more trouble today after what Mrs Fernsby said to her earlier. Even she isn't that stupid.'

'Are you sure about that?' Libby said.

Willow noticed what they were looking at and the worry in her eyes was obvious.

'We all just need to eat our food and drink our drinks and pretend we haven't seen them,' Ava suggested. She spooned a dollop of mash in her mouth and beckoned the others to do the same. 'Tuck in.'

'I think I've lost my appetite,' Libby said. But she followed suit.

Willow, on the other hand, just sat hunched over her dinner, her face flushed red with worry.

Spooning another dollop of mash in her mouth, Ava once again tried to encourage her to join in – to no avail. *Jeez, this is going to be even harder work than I thought it would be,*

Ava thought. 'There's no lumpy bits, which makes a nice change,' she said in an attempt to lighten the mood.

'It's still not too late to move to another table, you know,' Libby whispered in her ear. 'Although Ruth just glared at us, so maybe it is too late.'

Ava continued trying to make small talk with Willow. 'So, where have you moved here from?' she asked her. 'And why? Is it from far away? Is it to do with an irresistible job offer that one of your parents just couldn't say no to? Or were you forced to seek out cheaper digs in a less well-off area due to your family falling on hard times? Or ... is it just because your mum and dad saw a bargain must-have property and had to go for it – even if it meant *you* having to relocate to another school when you probably didn't want to? Got to be one of those reasons, yeah? And I hope it wasn't the last one, because I'd be *so* angry if I was put in that position.'

The new girl was seemingly too concerned about the location of the new arrivals to concentrate on answering intrusive questions. But then she did give a response.

'It was none of those reasons,' she said, her voice strained with emotion. 'We moved here because I was being bullied at my last school. And now I'm being bullied at this one.'

'Why were you bullied at your last school?' Libby asked. 'And why were things allowed to get so bad that your family had to move to another area? Didn't the teachers do anything about it? Or the head? Did he or she punish those responsible?'

'Of course she did,' Willow responded with a jittery edge to her voice. 'And it just made things worse.'

'And I bet it was just the one girl who was responsible for making your life hell, wasn't it?' Ava said.

'Pretty much,' Willow confirmed. 'But her friends taunted me every chance they got as well.'

'And now you've got her on your back,' Ava said, nodding toward Ruth, who was nearly done with her food selections.

'Yes, and now I've got *her* on my back,' Willow said, following her gaze. Willow looked as if she could burst into tears at any second. Her hand shook as she picked up her fork and repositioned it on her plate.

'You should talk to the headmistress if she's bothering you that much,' Libby advised.

'No, that's not what she should do,' Ava said. 'She needs to do what Mr Jones has done – and that's stand up for herself. He's the biggest wet lettuce of a teacher I've ever come across. If he can do it, then so can you. It's all about gritting your teeth and making a stand – no matter how scared you feel. Ruth won't give you any problems if she thinks you've got a spine. Libby, why are you looking at me like that? What's your problem?'

'Since when have you ever stood up to Ruth?' she responded. 'You need to take your own advice and grit your teeth and make a stand when she has a go at you. And, yes, so do I – before you state the obvious.'

For a second Ava stared open-mouthed at her friend. And then she scraped her foot down Libby's shin.

Libby screeched out an *'Ow!'*, which echoed around the hall, attracting unwanted attention. The kids on the nearby tables stopped what they were doing and gawked.

'Why did you do that?' Libby hissed at Ava.

'Why?' she responded through gritted teeth. 'Because I'm trying to inspire Willow to stick up for herself and you have to go and say something that really isn't going to help with the situation. Why don't you just use your brain for once before opening your mouth?'

'You didn't need to scrape me that hard!' Libby said, glaring at her. 'Perhaps I should scrape you back so you know what it's like!'

'You dare and I'll ... I'll throw my drink all over you,' Ava threatened.

'And then I'll throw my drink all over *you!*' Libby responded.

Their chairs scraped across the floor as they both stood up at the same time and grabbed their drinks. They stared at each other, making threats with their eyes, oblivious to what was going on around them.

'Erm, you pair,' Willow said, looking up at them, 'you might want to sit down because I think you're attracting unwanted attention.'

'And what unwanted attention might that be?' a familiar voice said. 'I hope you're not referring to me.'

Ava turned to see that Ruth and Amy were standing next to her.

Lost for words, Ava just stared at them, wishing that she

could somehow spirit herself away to another part of the school.

'You lot opted for the pie, I see,' Ruth said. 'I had that last week and I'm sorry to tell you that it wasn't that great.' She nodded at her own tray. 'You should have gone for the pizza. I've already had a nibble and it's super yummy.'

Ava was furious with herself for allowing Ruth to sneak up on them unnoticed. She didn't know what to say in response, so she just smiled.

'Thanks for letting us know about the pizza,' Libby said, smiling as well. 'We'll go for that next time.'

Ruth turned her attention to Willow. 'These your new friends, are they?' she asked her. 'Your new buddies?'

Willow opened her mouth to respond, but no words came out. She just stared up at her tormentor, the fear all too obvious in her eyes.

'She just asked you a question,' Amy said, nodding toward her friend. 'It'd be rude not to answer.'

When Willow didn't respond, just continued to stare, Ava chirped in with an explanation: 'She's quite shy and nervous because she was bullied at her last school. That's why she's here. To get away from being bullied. To make a new start.'

'And why was she bullied at her last school?' Amy asked, directing her question as much at Willow as she did at Ava, who wasn't sure how to respond.

'Because she's quiet and an easy target, I'm guessing,' Ava said. She realized she'd put her foot in it as soon as the words had left her mouth.

Ruth's eyes narrowed as she glared at her. 'Is that some sort of indirect accusation at us?' she said. 'Are you accusing us of picking on her?' she nodded at Willow, 'because she's quiet and an easy target? Is that what you're saying, Greenwood?'

Ava was quick to shake her head. 'No, no, that's not what I'm saying at all. You asked why she was forced to leave her last school, so I told you why. Look, none of us wants any trouble here, especially Willow. She's been through a lot recently and needs a break from any nastiness.'

'Nastiness?' Ruth said to her. 'Just exactly who's being nasty here? We've come over to talk to you and you're throwing all sorts of accusations at us. I'd say that *you're* the ones who're being nasty.'

'You haven't come over to talk to us,' Libby said in a surprisingly forceful tone, 'you've come to cause trouble like you always do. What was your plan? To accidentally spill your drink over one of us or something? Or were going to park yourself on a nearby table, throw food at us and then blame it on someone else? Or ... were you just planning on insulting us and having a good old laugh-fest?'

'Well, we could do all three,' Amy said, 'if that's what you want?'

'What we want is for you to leave us alone and go away,' Libby said.

'And if we don't,' Ruth said, taking a step forward, 'what are you going to do about it – eh?'

Libby locked eyes with Ruth, sending her a clear message.

'Wow!' Amy said, looking genuinely surprised but not the least bit concerned. 'Looks like someone's cruising for a bruising!'

Ava felt nothing short of terrified. But she puffed herself up in an attempt to look unintimidated. Any second now she was sure that a fist would come winging at her head …

Ava put down her drink to free up her hands and Libby followed suit.

'Double wow!' Amy exclaimed. She nodded at Willow. 'Do you want to stand up as well? Or are you comfortable down there, cringing in your seat?'

Willow stayed seated with her hands balled in her lap and a look of severe concern on her face.

'We're sticking at a double wow, then, I guess,' Amy said in a disappointed tone.

'Please just go away,' Libby said, 'and leave us alone.'

'No,' Ruth said. 'I'm detecting a lot of negativity here and I think that needs to be addressed. 'She motioned for Willow to get up. 'You can sit on the other side with your new friends and we can sit on this side. Then we can all have a nice, cozy chat and thrash things out. Won't *that* be nice?' Ruth slid Willow's tray across the table, causing her drink to fall over and spill everywhere.

Willow let out a screech as it seeped over the edge of the table and onto her lap. As she stood up, the back of her legs hit her chair and knocked it over.

'You cow!' Libby said. 'You did that on purpose!'

Ruth did her best to look insulted by such an accusation.

'It was an accident,' she protested. 'I was just trying to move her tray out of the way so I can put mine down.'

'Yeah, right, pull the other one!' Ava blurted.

'Are you calling me a liar?' Ruth said.

'I'm pretty sure she is,' Amy said.

Close to tears, Willow picked up her bag and stormed off, stamping her feet in frustration.

'She looks like she's peed herself!' Ruth said in a loud voice.

Amy burst out laughing.

'Why do you have to be so horrible?' Libby asked Ruth.

She shrugged and grinned. 'I dunno,' she said, 'it's just a talent that I have.'

Ava could see that Libby was balling her hand into a fist and thought: *oh no, please don't do anything silly; this will NOT end well for us*. Ava tried to get her attention, but Libby was too focused on glaring at Ruth to notice anyone else.

Silence had descended in the hall as everyone was now focused on the spectacle that was playing out.

'I think you need to run after your friend and see if she's okay,' Amy suggested to Ava and Libby, 'don't you? It was only a bit of drink that got spilled down her front, so I'm sure she'll be okay.'

'Oh, really?' Libby said. 'You think so?' She picked up her own drink and threw it down Amy's front.

A look of shock spread across her face as all the onlookers let out hoots of approval.

'Have you got a death wish?' Ruth asked Libby.

'It's just a bit of drink,' Libby replied with a smile playing at the corners of her mouth. 'I'm sure she'll be okay.'

Ava leaned in close to her and whispered in her ear: 'Now might be a good time to run.'

And that's what they would have done had it not been for the loud voice which echoed across the room to them. They all turned to see Miss Becker, the English teacher, striding toward them.

'I saw that!' she said, glaring at Libby.

Like the headmistress, Miss Becker was not a teacher to be messed with. Her voice boomed when she spoke, even when she wasn't angry. She was a stocky woman with a thick neck and shoulder-length dark hair which framed her wide face. Her bulbous top lip curled into a snarl as she took in the situation before her, weighing things up.

'They started it,' Libby explained, nodding at Ruth. 'And she knocked a drink over Willow on purpose. She'll tell you that it was an accident, but it *wasn't*.'

'It *was* an accident!' Ruth said, doing her best to look coy and innocent.

Miss Becker held her hands up, quietening the girls. She looked at Ruth and Amy, then shook her head. 'I might have known that you two would be involved. Nearly every time there's trouble, you're at the center of it. I didn't see this "accident" take place, so I can't say for sure whether it was intentional.' She turned her attention to Libby. 'But I *did* see you throw your drink over Amy, which was not warranted – whether you were provoked or not.'

Libby nodded at Ruth. 'Please tell me that it's not just me you're going to punish and that she's not going to get away with drenching Willow.'

'There's a certain way to respond to these things and you made a bad choice,' Miss Becker explained. 'You should have found a teacher and told them about the situation. Perhaps next time you'll engage your brain before lashing out.' She turned her attention to Amy. 'And as for you, think yourself lucky that I didn't walk in the room a minute earlier. I'm quite confident you wouldn't be dodging a bullet if that were the case. But, as things stand, I just want you to get out of my sight and get yourself cleaned up.'

Amy gestured toward her skirt, which was soaked through at the front. 'And how exactly am I supposed to clean *this* up?'

'I'm sure you'll figure it out,' Miss Becker said. 'But if I were you, I'd try the heated blowers in the toilets. You can angle the head downwards on those things, so that should do the trick.'

As Amy and Ruth were walking away, they sent some dirty looks at Ava and Libby to tell them that their business wasn't finished.

'Your detention will be on Friday,' Miss Becker informed Libby. 'After school. Room 34. Do *not* be late.' She walked away before Libby could voice any protest.

'Great!' she said when she was satisfied that she was out of earshot. 'They start the trouble and I end up with a detention. Where's the justice?'

'Oh well,' Ava said, 'at least Amy got drenched. Did you see the look on her face when you did it? If I could get a picture of that, I'd put it on my bedroom wall so I could have a good laugh at her every day.'

'It was a spur-of-the-moment thing. I don't regret it. And you don't need to tell me what trouble it will have caused. They'll be gunning for us, so we need to be ready. Why is everyone still gawking at us? I don't like it when people stare at me.'

'It's because we just put on a show. Come on, let's get out of here. Let's try and find Willow.'

'But what about our food?'

'I've lost my appetite.'

Libby looked down at her tray of food and shook her head. 'Yeah, I've lost mine too,' she said. 'What a waste.'

As they left the hall – with all eyes still on them – Libby said, 'So where do you think she'll have gone? I wouldn't be surprised if she's gone home, to be honest. That's what I'd have done.'

'It's either that or she'll have gone to the toilet.'

Both girls stopped and looked at each other as the same thing occurred to them.

'That's where Miss Becker had suggested that Amy should go to clean herself up,' Ava said.

'Uh-oh, this could be bad. Very bad – for Willow.'

The nearest toilet was at the end of the corridor, so that's where they jogged toward. But as they were nearing the door, Libby grabbed Ava by her arm and pulled her to a stop.

'Just hang on a minute,' Libby said in a low voice, 'maybe we should think about this before bursting in there. We don't really know the new girl, so why are we rushing to help her? Wouldn't we be better off finding Miss Becker or some other teacher and telling them about it? Why put ourselves in the firing line?'

'We're already in the firing line,' Ava pointed out. 'Or have you forgotten about what just happened in the dining hall? If you were in Willow's position, wouldn't you want someone to come and help? And I don't see any teachers around, do you? By the time we find one, it'll probably be too late.'

'There are six toilets in this school. Who's to say that they're in there?'

'Well, this is the nearest one. And there's only one way to find out.'

Ava led the way and Libby followed her reluctantly. As they neared the door they heard voices echoing inside the room:

'This'll teach you to mess with us ...'

Not wasting a second, Ava burst through the door to find Ruth and Amy crowded in a cubicle door, with a pair of legs jutting out above them.

'What the hell are you doing?' Ava demanded to know.

'We're flushing this rat's head down the toilet,' Amy said with a big grin on her face.

'Let her go,' Libby said with no force in her voice.

'We will do in a minute,' Ruth said, 'when we've finished with her.' She and Amy pushed as hard as they could, trying to get Willow's head into the pan.

Willow let out a stifled, choking scream.

'Let her go now or we're going to get the headmistress,' Ava threatened. 'You're already in her bad books so you'll probably get a week's worth of detentions for this. Or you could be suspended. How are you going to explain *that* to your parents?'

Ruth loosened her grip on Willow and then told Amy to do the same. As soon as Willow was lowered back onto her feet, she snatched up her bag and fled the room with tears in her eyes.

'Well thanks for ruining our fun,' Amy said, scowling at Ava and Libby.

'Maybe we should flush your heads down the bog instead,' Ruth suggested, eyeing them up. 'Who wants to be first?'

Even though it would be two versus two, Ava still didn't like the odds. She didn't like the idea of having her head flushed down a toilet either. And neither did Libby, judging by the look on her face.

Ruth took a step forward and that was enough to get them moving.

Ava and Libby bolted. Reaching the door first, Ava yanked it open and then both girls got stuck shoulder-to-shoulder for a second as they attempted to exit at the same time.

'*Grrrrr!*' Libby said in frustration. '*What the heck!*'

Spewing into the corridor, they heard cries of rage behind them as they took off toward the south wing, pushing their way past other students.

'Where shall we go?' Ava said, panicking wildly.

'We need to find a teacher!' Libby responded. She led the way up a stairwell and, as Ava followed, she figured out where they were going: the staffroom.

'There's no point in running!' Amy called up to them. 'We're going to catch up with you eventually, so you may as well just face us now!'

Exiting on the second floor, Libby continued to take the lead as they made their way quickly down another corridor.

'All for a girl we don't even know and who's run off when we tried to help her,' she said. She was about to knock on the door, but then …

'Wait! Don't do that!'

They turned to see the bullies advancing along the corridor toward them.

'Don't do that,' Ruth said again. 'We weren't going to hurt her – it was just a bit of fun, that's all. You don't need to dob us in.'

'A bit of fun?' Libby said. 'Did you see the look on Willow's face when she fled the toilet? Did it look like *she* was having fun?'

'No,' Ruth said. 'It didn't.'

'She was terrified,' Ava said. 'And you two were laughing about it.'

'We were,' Ruth admitted.

'And do you have any idea where she could be?' Libby said. 'Because we don't. She could have legged it out of the school and be anywhere for all we know.'

The staffroom door opened and Mr Shaw stepped out. He looked at the girls with raised eyebrows. 'What's going on here then?' he said. 'Having a friendly powwow, are we?'

'Yes,' Ruth said, piping in before anyone else could speak, 'that's exactly what we're doing.'

Libby gawped at her through narrowed eyes. Ava was sure that she was about to spew a different version of events, but then Libby's expression softened and she said, 'Yes, we're having a friendly powwow.'

'Well, that's good to hear,' Mr Shaw said sarcastically. He closed the door and added: 'But why are you actually gathered here? Outside the staffroom? Is there something I can help you with? Have you come to sign up for the charity fundraiser next month so you can help out? You want me to put all of your names down, yes?'

'No!' Amy was quick to respond. 'I'll take a pass on that one, thanks.'

All the other girls declined as well.

'But you'll be there to show your support, yes?' Mr Shaw inquired.

They all nodded.

'There'll be stalls and games, so it sounds like it could be fun,' Ruth said.

'It will be,' Mr Shaw said. 'But not one of you has answered my initial question, so I'll ask it again: why are you outside this staffroom? You should either be in the playground or dinner hall, not here.'

All the girls looked at each other – and then Libby came up with a plausible explanation: 'We were playing dob,' she explained. 'And it's my fault we ended up here. I ran up the stairs and the others followed.'

Mr Shaw did not look convinced, but he shooed the students away anyway.

Ava and Libby moved away slowly to give the other two a chance to disappear before they began making their way down the stairwell.

'Do you think we did the right thing not dobbing in Ruth and Amy just now?' Libby said.

'Yeah, I think so. Who knows, maybe they'll feel like they owe us one because of that and won't give us any grief from now on. What do you think?'

This question was asked tongue in cheek by Ava and got the response she'd expected: a resounding no.

'Not a cat in hell's chance,' Libby added with a chuckle.

'So where do you think Willow will have gone this time?' Libby said.

'Well, I don't think it'll be one of the toilets.'

'No, I don't either.' Libby checked the time on her watch. 'Break ends in fifteen minutes, so we could do with finding her as soon as possible.'

Ava clicked her fingers together as she mulled over the possibilities.

'We can't check the upper floors because we're bound to run into a teacher,' Libby said. 'Probably Mr Shaw, knowing our luck. And I can't think of an explanation for us being up there. Can you?'

Ava shook her head.

'What about the bike sheds?' Libby suggested. 'D'you think she could be there?'

'Probably not. But we may as well take a look. It's somewhere to start, at least.'

They managed to do a thorough check of all the outside areas before the bell rang to sound the end of dinner time – but they just couldn't find her.

'What's her next lesson?' Ava said to Libby. 'Do you know?'

She shrugged. 'No idea. But she does have her last lesson with me.'

'We'll just have to wait and see if she turns up for that.'

'I'd suggest telling a teacher that we're concerned about her, but then we'd have to answer some awkward questions: ones that would drop Ruth and Amy in it and make things even worse than they already are.'

'Let's just wait until the last lesson,' Ava said, watching all the other students make their way back toward the building. 'We may have to say something if we haven't come across her by then.'

'If she's missing from her next lesson, the teacher will raise concerns about her whereabouts. So we probably won't even need to say anything, if that's the case.'

'I'd like to say that she'll be fine, but Ruth and Amy tried to flush her head down the bog, so she's probably about as far from fine as she could be.'

'Yeah, that'd mess my head up, for sure. I would have run straight home after that. And that's probably what she's done.'

'I'd have run home, too. But we still need to keep an eye out for her, just in case.'

'Oh, I will – don't worry about that. Come on, let's get moving before a teacher yells at us.'

As they were making their way across the playground, they saw a girl ahead of them trip over and fall flat on her face.

'Ouch!' Libby said, grimacing. 'Now that *had* to have hurt.'

'Definitely,' Ava agreed.

They watched as the girl's friends crowded around her and helped her back to her feet. Blood was gushing from her nose, staining her white shirt crimson. The initial look of shock that'd been on her face had been replaced by one which suggested a mixture of embarrassment and pain. Tears were now streaming down her cheeks as a teacher shepherded her inside the door.

'I feel like that's the sort of thing that'd happen to me,' Libby mused.

'Don't say something like that,' Ava said. 'You're tempting fate ...'

'There's no such thing as fate.'

'You're probably right – but I still wouldn't risk it.'

4.

The next lesson proved to be an eventful one. Geography was Ava's favorite subject – and not just because she liked learning about the world. Not only did she get to sit with her best friend, but there were also no bullies to worry about.

Things started as normal with Mr Case telling everyone what they would be studying for the next fifty or so minutes. He was a very animated teacher, who was always walking back and forth at the front of class. Rarely would you find him seated and it was never for long. He wasn't a strict teacher, but he did command the respect of every student because he was so well-liked.

And so when he leaned against his wooden desk and it collapsed sideways, there was no outcry of laughter as he went crashing down with it, a shocked look on his face. A moment of silence followed as he quickly got back to his feet and brushed himself off. He looked at the students and they looked at him. And that's when the laughter erupted, led by Mr Case himself as he began guffawing uncontrollably while clutching at his stomach to catch his breath.

'Now why can't something like that happen to Mrs Fernsby,' Libby said to Ava.

'She wouldn't laugh about it; she'd be angry as hell.'

'Damn right she would.'

Mr Case appealed for calm, taking deep breaths to try to get himself under control. 'Well, that was a bit of a surprise, wasn't it?' he said, looking down at the crumpled mess that used to be his desk. 'Now, who'll volunteer to help me clean this up?'

Silence descended.

Mr Case made a sad face. 'What? No one? Are you really going to let me do this on my own?'

Ava got up and then so did Libby. A few others joined them. It didn't take long for the mess to be moved to the side, out of the way.

Mr Case thanked the helpers and then said, 'Hopefully I won't get charged for that.'

He took a spare seat from the back and resumed the lesson. Everything sailed along normally – until five minutes before the end. A boy named Gareth had been told that he could select a book from the wall-mounted shelf. He was perusing along the line of books when one end somehow became unsecured and the whole thing swung downward like a guillotine. A thick, heavy hardback landed on Gareth's foot, causing him to yelp out in pain. Everyone looked on in shock as he collapsed dramatically to the floor like a football player looking for a penalty.

'What on earth!' Mr Case said as he moved quickly across the room to see if he was okay.

'It's broken!' Gareth said, rolling around in apparent agony. '*Eeeeee!* It's broken!'

Mr Case beckoned him to stay still and told him to keep calm. 'It probably isn't,' he said, 'so I wouldn't worry too much.' He helped him up and seated him on the nearest chair. 'Right, let's get your shoe and sock off and take a gander.'

As it turned out, Gareth had no broken metatarsals or

phalanges. His only injury was a slight bruising of his big toe (his ego had taken more of a bashing than his body, it seemed).

After giving him the all-clear to walk again, Mr Case went to inspect the shelf and where it'd been secured to the wall. He was looking rather puzzled, scratching the side of his head, as the bell sounded and everyone began to leave the room.

'A loose screw or two?' Ava said to him as she was packing away her books.

'No, that'll be you,' Libby said to her with a cheeky smile.

'Ha-ha – very funny,' Ava responded.

Mr Case was still puzzled. 'I put this shelf up about a week ago and I secured it properly,' he said, 'so I don't see how this could have happened. Unless …'

'Someone loosened the screws?' Ava said, finishing his sentence. 'For a joke.'

'A joke that could have got someone badly injured,' Libby noted.

'Someone was badly injured,' Ava said, 'if Gareth's reaction to that book dropping on his foot was anything to go by.'

Mr Case sighed as he looked down at the mess of books on the floor and then over at the crumpled mess that used to be his desk. 'Anyone would think we had a riot in here,' he said, managing a smile.

'We can help you pick up the books if you like?' Libby said.

'Thanks for the offer,' Mr Case said, 'but you'll be late for your next lesson and I can handle this.'

Ava and Libby left him to it and hurried up to the next floor.

'Do you think she'll be there?' Ava said to Libby as they exited the stairwell and made their way along the corridor

'There's only one way to find out,' she replied.

They arrived at room 54 and peered into the classroom. Willow was sitting at the front, so she was easy to pick out. She noticed that her friends were looking at her and averted her gaze. She looked sheepish and troubled, which was to be expected, after what'd happened to her in the toilet.

'She looks pale and unwell,' Ava noted.

'You would too if you'd nearly had your head flushed down the pan,' Libby said. 'I'll try and talk to her. See what she has to say.'

'Okay,' Ava said, 'but you won't be able to get much out of her during the lesson. We need to talk to her properly. If we get to the gates before her at home time, we can walk with her and powwow. Agreed?'

'Agreed,' Libby said.

They fist-bumped each other and then Ava set off for her class, which she was now going to be late for. Great. She hurried up to the next floor and was slightly out of breath when she arrived. She knew that she would be stared at as she entered the classroom, so she took a second to steel herself. She took a deep breath. She peered through the glass in the door and saw that Mr Parkes was writing something on the whiteboard, scribbling away animatedly as he always did when he was deeply engrossed in his pontifications. *Oh my life, he is going to be* so *miffed with me*, Ava thought.

She opened the door, apologized for being late and offered up her explanation. Inevitably, Mr Parkes was not happy about having his maths lesson interrupted, so he gestured for her to take a seat as quickly as possible.

Ava made her way between the desks, focusing on nothing but her own, which was near the back. She was so focused on it that she didn't notice a pale, white slab of a leg shoot out in front of her.

After that, everything felt like it was happening in slow motion – her eyes widening, her hands splaying out in front of her, the screeching exclamation of '*Ahhhhhh!*' that burst forth from her throat – until she went sprawling, her knees going down hard on the wooden floor. And then, of course, came the laughter – quickly followed by the angry voice of Mr Parkes, who wanted to know what was happening and why there'd been a sudden outburst of noise. His eyes fell upon Ava, who was just getting back to her feet. He glared at her, but she didn't notice. She was too busy doing some glaring of her own.

'Why are looking at me like that?' Ruth said with a smile playing at the corners of her mouth.

Ava opened her mouth intending to throw an accusation at her, but then she decided not to. Mr Parkes hadn't seen what'd happened and Ruth would only deny it, so there was no point. Ava was sure that no one in the class would back her up – not even the girl she sat next to all the time, Becky (who was kind of a friend).

'Did you just fall or did someone trip you?' Mr Parkes asked Ava. He looked at Ruth through narrowed eyes, then back at Ava, waiting impatiently for an answer. 'Well, has the cat got your tongue, or something, little miss?'

'I tripped,' Ava said, lowering her head in shame. 'I'm sorry. I should have been taking notice of where I was going.'

'Tripped, did you?' Mr Parkes said. He once again eyed Ruth through narrowed eyes, then turned his attention back to Ava. 'Are you hurt? If not, can you take your seat so I can get on with the remainder of this lesson?'

Ava took her seat.

Mr Parkes eyed everyone in the class. 'Any more interruptions,' he warned, his gaze lingering on Ruth for a second or two, 'and I will *not* be happy.' He turned back to face the whiteboard. 'Now, where was I?' he said, ready with his black marker. 'Ah, yes, I remember ...' He began scribbling again and was soon back in full flow.

Inevitably, Ruth could not resist a smirking glance back at Ava. And Amy, who was sitting next to Ruth, was smirking too.

Yeah, go on, laugh it up, Ava thought. *You'll get yours soon enough; you wait and see.*

As things turned out, Ava wasn't the only one to get laughed at in class. A boy called David bent over to pick something up and cracked his head on the side of his desk, which left a swelling above his eye. He looked close to tears as Mr Parkes examined his wound and told him that he'd live.

What is going on? Ava thought, remembering all the other mishaps that'd taken place since Willow had gone missing. *First the girl in the playground, then the two furniture disasters in Mr Case's class, and now* this. Ava shook her head and wondered what else could go wrong in what remained of the school day.

5.

At home time, Ava waited by the gates, leaning against the big oak tree which shadowed the entrance. She ducked out of sight when she saw Ruth and Amy striding toward her, laughing their heads off at something or other. She overheard what they were talking about and wasn't surprised to learn that she was the butt of their jokes.

'Did you see the look on her face as she went down?' Amy said. 'That hilarious expression she pulled?'

'I nearly peed myself with laughing!' Ruth exclaimed with a wild chuckle.

Ava waited until they were a safe distance away before breaking cover. She watched them through slitted eyes as they disappeared into the distance.

'Were you hiding behind that tree?' a familiar voice said.

Ava turned to see Willow and Libby approaching with quizzical looks on their faces.

'Yes, I was,' Ava said. 'And I'm sure I don't need to give

you two guesses as to who I was hiding from.'

'Eh, Ruth and Amy, by any chance?' Libby said.

'Bingo! Right the first time!'

'Been giving you trouble, have they?' Willow said.

Ava explained about what'd happened and how humiliated she had felt.

Screwing up her face in anger, Libby said, 'It's a good job I wasn't there; I'd have probably socked one of 'em in the eye.'

'And you'd have got a detention.' Ava said.

'It'd be worth it,' Libby replied. 'I've already got one this week, so why not go for the double?' She rolled her eyes to show that she was joking.

'You have a detention?' Willow said. 'Why?'

Libby explained what'd happened after Willow had fled from the dinner hall.

'That is *so* unfair,' Willow said, annoyed.

'Tell me about it,' Libby said. 'I'm still miffed.'

'We do need to deal with them pair, but we need to do it intelligently,' Ava said, 'as in not in a way that's going to get us in trouble.'

'And how would we do that?' Libby enquired.

Ava shrugged. 'No idea,' she said. 'Hopefully something will come to me.' She turned her attention to Willow. 'How are you feeling? Are you okay? Sorry, those are stupid questions, I know – but they're the sort of things you say to someone even when you know they're not all right, aren't they?'

'I'm about as good as I can be,' Willow said dejectedly,

'given everything that's happened to me since I started at this school.'

Ava noted that she still looked a little pale and unwell.

'We thought that you might have gone home,' Libby said, 'after that business in the toilet.'

'I came close to storming out of this place,' Willow admitted, 'but I dug my heels in and decided to stay. I figured that if I did leave then the idiots had won – that they'd beaten me. And I don't want that to be the case. That's the mistake I made at my last school. I can't make it again.'

'Now that's the attitude I want to see,' Libby said, giving her an encouraging pat on the arm.

'Yeah, that's the attitude,' Ava agreed. She noticed a girl walking past with a bandage on her arm and said, 'That's another one! What has been going on today? Why have so many kids hurt themselves?' She listed all the accidents and mishaps she'd witnessed and heard about.

'Mr Brookes slipped over in the second-floor corridor and did the splits, ripping his trousers around his crotch,' Libby said, smiling. 'I couldn't help but laugh. And some boys did too. I've never seen anyone go so red; I thought his head was going to explode when he yelled at us. And then, later on, Kerry Higham somehow managed to catch her fingernail on something and bent it back. Looked painful to me. She did well to hold back the tears as she was in some discomfort, I can tell you.'

Something occurred to Ava: 'There's been an abnormal amount of accidents ever since you went missing, Willow. It's probably just a coincidence, but ...' The guilty look on Willow's face suggested not. 'Is there something you want to tell us?'

Willow bit down on her bottom lip and looked close to bursting into tears.

'Hey, there's no way any of it could be your fault,' Libby said, putting an arm around her.

'But it is,' Willow admitted. She slid her bag off her back and unzipped it. She reached inside and gave them a glance at a book before stowing it back away.

Ava noted the title, written in gothic style gold lettering: *Shadowbound*. 'So you got a book? So what?'

'Elaboration, please!' Libby comically blurted at Willow.

'Okay, I better start at the beginning,' she said, She took a moment to compose herself before resuming: 'I love reading books. And so you can imagine how excited I was to discover that quirky book store, The Book Cove, in the town center. Have either of you been in there?' Willow didn't wait for a reply. 'It's an old-fashioned place with shelves stacked from the floor to the ceiling. I spent hours in there on Saturday, exploring *every* section on *every* floor. And it was on the top floor that I discovered this,' she said, tapping the side of her bag, 'in the magic and mysticism section, funnily enough. As soon as I clapped my eyes on it, I knew I had to have it. I felt drawn to it, for some reason. And, as weird as it sounds, I felt like it was drawn to me. When I went to pay for the book, the old man behind the counter told me that it'd been in the shop for about six months and that he was almost sad to see it go. And it was when I began reading through it that I found out why. In the preface, it says that only a witch or a wizard can cast the spells contained within. It also says no one will want to buy the book unless they're magical.' Willow let her last words hang in the air for her friends to draw conclusions from ...

Ava and Libby looked at each other. And then they looked at their friend.

'Are you trying to tell us that you're a witch and that all those accidents that have taken place are your fault?' Ava said.

'Yes,' Willow said simply. She bit down on her lip again, very sheepish.

'Magic isn't real,' Libby said.

Willow replied: 'I can prove it.'

'Do it,' Libby said, rolling her eyes at Ava.

'Okay,' Willow said. 'The simplest spell is the levitation one.' She looked around, casing out the area, and then pointed to a black plastic bin near the building. 'I make that float if you like? There aren't many people around now, so I doubt anyone will notice.'

Libby and Ava, looking rather amused and doubtful, gestured for her to go ahead.

Putting her bag on the floor, Willow pulled her book out and began skimming through it ...

Ava noted the title again and said, '*Shadowbound*. Sounds ominous.' She also noted that there was no author's name on the front cover.

Libby agreed: 'Yep – deffo ominous.'

Meanwhile, Willow had found the page she was looking for. She ran her finger along a line and then fixed all her concentration on the bin: 'Suspendus Levitatus!'

Ava and Libby watched in amazement as the bin began to float in the air, about a foot above the tarmac.

'*Whoa!*' Ava said, gob-smacked.

'That can't be real!' Libby said. 'It's a trick, right?'

A girl came hopping and skipping out of school and then stopped dead in her tracks when she noticed the bin.

Willow let it drop back to the tarmac with a clatter.

'Uh-oh, this could take some explaining,' Libby said.

'Just don't look at her,' Willow said. 'And if she asks if we saw anything, just say no.'

The girl was examining the bin with a curious expression on her face. She picked it up, looked underneath it, then put it back down. She looked very confused as she cast several troubled glances back toward the bin on her way to the gate.

She looked over at the girls as if she were about to say something, but then she carried on along the pavement until she was out of sight.

'She'll convince herself that she imagined it,' Willow assured the other two.

'What if she tells someone,' Ava said.

'They'll probably just think that she's joking,' Willow said. 'Either way, they won't believe her. As Libby said: Magic isn't real.'

'And yet you just made a bin float.' Ava noted.

'I still think it's a trick,' Libby said. 'It *has* to be.'

Willow looked at her and said the magical words …

Ava gasped in amazement as her friend began floating above the ground. Libby, on the other hand, looked terrified.

'All right, yeah – okay!' she said, her eyes wide with shock. 'You've made your point! You can put me down now!'

Willow lowered her back down.

'Oh my frickin' frick,' Ava said, laughing her head off. 'Did that really just happen? Did it?'

'Yes, it did,' Libby said, looking around to see if anyone had witnessed her spell in the air.

Ava noticed two boys walking across the playground, but they were too engrossed in exchanging some sort of cards to be aware of anything else around them.

Ava noticed something else, too. All the color had drained from Willow's face and she looked as if she might throw up.

'Are you okay?' Libby asked her.

Willow leaned against the tree for support. 'Yeah … well, no,' she said, clearly in discomfort. 'I just need a minute to rest and then I think I'll be okay.'

'Is that because you did those spells?' Ava said.

'I'm not sure,' she replied, 'but I did feel quite sick after doing the spell to make everyone in the school susceptible to being accident-prone.'

'When you say everyone,' Libby said, 'did that include us?'

'No, I excluded you pair,' Willow said, slumping down the tree. 'Oh gawd, I really could do with resting properly.'

Ava looked around for somewhere to seat her friend. The

wall by the gate was the best that she could see. She and Libby helped her over to it and stood watching her while she rested.

'Will this happen every time you do a spell?' Libby said.

'I have no idea,' Willow said, looking a little better now that she'd taken the weight off her feet.

'Well, it seems like too much of a coincidence for me,' Ava said. 'You felt like crap after doing that first spell and now you feel even worse. Does it say anything in the book about there being any side effects?'

'Not that I've noticed,' Willow replied. 'But then it is quite chunky.'

'You need to be careful where that book is concerned,' Ava said. 'I mean, the title alone should be enough to set alarm bells ringing. Don't you think?'

Libby nodded. But Willow just shrugged.

'Are you feeling any better yet?' Libby asked her.

'Yeah, a bit,' Willow replied. 'I'll be okay after some rest, I think; I feel like I've been drained and that I just need to recharge.'

Ava and Libby exchanged knowing looks with each other.

'The old man said that the book had been in the shop for some time,' Libby said, 'so how come someone else hasn't bought it? Someone else who's magical? Someone else who's a witch or wizard?'

Willow opened her mouth to reply, but Ava beat her to it. 'Perhaps there aren't many magical people about – maybe one in a hundred, or a thousand, or something. That would explain why it'd been there for so long.'

Willow said, 'It says in the preface that magical people are not very common. It also says that non-magical people won't see the preface. All they will see is a blank page.'

Libby held her hand out and said, 'Can I take a look?'

Willow gave her head a slight shake as she clutched her bag protectively to her belly.

'Oh, come on,' Libby said, 'I'm not going to steal it from you. I just want to take a quick gander and then I'll give it straight back. You have my word.'

Reluctantly, Willow took the book out of her bag, handed it over, then watched as Libby thumbed through the first few pages.

'So where is this preface then?' Libby asked.

Willow helped her find the correct page.

'I see nothing but a blank sheet of old, discolored paper,' Libby said.

'And that's all I see too,' Ava said, 'so I guess neither of us are witches then. I'm not going to lie, I'm disappointed.'

'Me, too,' Libby said.

Seeing that Willow wasn't comfortable being separated from her book, Ava took it from Libby and handed it back.

'I'm sorry to sound so skeptical,' Libby said, 'but I just find it a bit of a stretch that you could be an actual witch. I mean, a *real* witch? Come on!'

'After everything that's happened?' Ava said. 'The accidents? The levitations? How can you be skeptical about anything? Have you already forgotten about what she just did to you?'

'No, of course I haven't forgotten,' Libby said. 'It's just that ...' She shook her head as she eyed Willow warily. 'These sorts of things don't happen in real life. People don't cast spells to make others have accidents and levitation is the stuff of fantasy. And witches and wizards and spell books aren't real – or so I thought.'

'Taking everything into consideration,' Ava said, 'I think we just need to accept that Willow is one – don't you?'

'Yeah ... yeah, I guess,' Libby said, still not looking convinced. 'But where's your wand?' she asked Willow.

'I don't need one,' she replied as she stood up.

'I think you should rest for a bit longer,' Ava suggested. 'You still don't look too great.'

'My mum will chew my ear off if I get home late without telling her that I was going to be late,' Willow said, throwing her bag over her shoulder. 'Look, I've reversed the accident spell, so there's nothing to worry about there. It will all be back to normal tomorrow and everyone will be able to carry on as they were.'

'Can we have your phone number and address?' Ava asked her. 'Just in case you don't show up tomorrow? If you're off ill then we can ring you up to see if you're okay or pop round and pay you a visit, yeah?'

Willow scribbled on a piece of paper and folded it up. She handed it over and said, 'Just don't call after eight in the evening – otherwise you'll experience my mum's wrath.' She began walking toward the gate.

'Make sure you get plenty of rest this evening,' Ava said, watching her with a worried expression.

'And don't do any more magic until you feel better!' Libby advised.

'Keep your voice down!' Ava chided.

Willow raised a hand as she disappeared through the gate and made her way across the street.

Ava and Libby watched her until she was out of sight.

Unfolding the note, Ava saw that Willow had written down an address but not a phone number.

Then Libby said, 'What the actual hell is going on? Am I dreaming this, or what? No way can she be a real witch. And no way did she make all those people have accidents and make me float in the air. No frickin' way!'

'And yet she did,' Ava said simply.

'Yeah – but look at the state of her after doing only a few spells. Imagine what she'll be like in a week, or a month, or a year. That's assuming she'd still be alive in a year.'

'We can't be sure that doing magic is what's done that to her. She might have a virus or something. It could be stress that's brought it on. I mean, she has had a pretty stressful day, hasn't she? Ruth and Amy tried to flush her head in the toilet. That alone would make me ill.'

'Yeah, me too. But my instincts are telling me that the book is the problem. It's making alarm bells ring in my skull. Ya get it?'

Ava nodded. She got it.

'So what are we going to do about it?' Libby said.

'We need to find out as much as we can about that book. And that means a trip to the place where she got it from. Mr Grimes, who owns the place, might be able to tell us something.'

'And when do you think we should do that?'

'Well I'm not doing anything this afternoon, so …'

'We'll need to let our parents know. And we don't know what time the shop closes, so it may be shut by the time we get there.'

'Most shops close at five, so I think we'll make it in time.'

The girls arranged to meet at the shop in half an hour and then set off along the main road at a brisk pace.

6.

The shop, an old Victorian building, was in the center of town, tucked down a side street. A bell above the door tinkled as the girls entered. The counter was to the left, but there was nobody behind it. The place consisted of three floors, all crammed with tall bookcases. Every inch of space was taken up by books: piled up here and there, crammed into any nook that would take them. The atmosphere was dusty and a strong scent of incense was always the first thing to assault the senses.

'I'm amazed at how he's got so many books into this place,' Libby said, perusing the shelves. 'And I'm curious as to where he gets them from.' She picked one up titled *A Travelers' Guide to Italy* and began thumbing through the pages. 'I've always wanted to go to Italy. Some amazing sights to see there.'

'Forget the sights,' Ava said, 'let's just concentrate on finding the old man so we can ask him some questions.'

'And what questions would those be?' a gruff voice said.

The girls turned to see that Mr Grimes was now standing behind the counter. A short, old man with a bald head, he regarded his customers with a curious look, his bushy eyebrows raised inquisitively.

'Oh, hello,' Ava said, slightly taken aback by his sudden appearance. 'We didn't see you there.'

'Evidently not,' Mr Grimes responded chirpily. His eyebrows were still raised, asking a question without asking a question.

'You recently sold a book to one of our friends,' Libby said, making her way toward the counter, 'and we'd like to know if you can remember anything about the book and how you got hold of it.'

'What's the title and when did your friend buy it?' Mr Grimes enquired. 'If it was more than a week or two ago then you'll be out of luck. My memory is not what it used to be, I'm afraid. One of the many downsides of getting old. I quite often walk into a room these days and have no idea why I'm there.' He let out a little chuckle and smiled.

Ava told him the title. 'And she would have bought it very recently as she's new to the area.'

She considered adding a description of Willow, but there was no need. A look of recognition had spread across Mr

Grime's wizened face.

'Ah, yes,' he said. 'I remember her. A very pleasant girl. Softly spoken. Eager to make her purchase and be gone, for some reason. And as for the book, I was surprised to see it appear here on the counter. I didn't think I'd ever get rid of it, what with it having a dull cover and, shall we say, questionable content. I mean, what does a young girl want with a book about dark magic? Not that magic is real, of course. But, still ...' Mr Grimes shrugged his bony shoulders.

'Willow is ... into odd things,' Ava said, letting out a little chuckle of her own.

'You want to know how I came by the book,' Mr Grimes said, 'but I'm going to have to ask the obvious question of why?'

Ava looked at Libby, who just stared back at her with a blank expression.

'We just wondered if you ... might have another copy,' Ava said, making something up on the spot.

'I only had one, I'm afraid,' Mr Grimes said. He looked from one girl to the other, eyeing them with a suspicious expression. 'So why do you want to know how I came by it? And don't give me any hogwash about wanting another copy, because I pride myself on being able to detect lies. I'd rather you were just honest with me. It'll save us all time if you just get to the point.'

The girls looked at each other again ...

It was Libby who spoke up this time. 'Our friend Willow has been acting strange ever since she got hold of that book,' she explained. 'Let's just say that we don't think that it's having a positive influence on her and we'd like to talk to the previous owner to see if he or she has had a similar experience.'

'Not been a positive influence?' Mr Grimes said. 'Can you elaborate?'

Not without it sounding daft, Ava thought.

'Well, it's a book about dark magic,' Libby said, 'so we think it's … casting a dark shadow over Willow, somehow.'

'A dark shadow?' Mr Grimes said, once again eyeing the girls suspiciously. 'What sort of "dark shadow"? Can you stop talking around what it is that you really want to say and just blurt it out? I have new stock to sort through and I'd like to get it done before I close, thank you very much.'

The sound of descending footsteps made everyone look toward the stairs. A few seconds later a woman appeared, clutching a handful of books. Ava and Libby moved out of the way so she could place her purchases on the counter.

'Ah, some excellent thrillers there!' Mr Grimes said, surveying the books before him. 'And enough to keep you going for some time.'

While he was distracted, Ava grabbed Libby by the arm and led her out of earshot.

'I wouldn't tell him anything about what happened at school today,' Ava whispered to her. 'He'll just think that we're either mad or trying to pull some sort of prank on him.'

'I wasn't going to say anything like that,' Libby whispered

back. 'But what are we going to say about why we want to know where he got the book?'

Ava did some quick thinking. 'We could tell him … that we found something inside the book – something valuable – and that we'd like to return it to the previous owner.'

'And what is this valuable something?'

Ava shrugged. 'Pfff – I dunno – some money. A twenty-pound note, perhaps.'

Libby thought about this for a moment and then nodded. 'Yeah, that'll work – maybe. This guy prides himself on being able to detect lies, though, remember?'

'Well, we'll just have to hope he doesn't detect this one, 'cause I can't think of anything else. Can you?'

Libby shook her head. 'No.'

The bell above the door tinkled as the woman exited the shop.

Looking toward the counter, Ava saw that Mr Grimes was once again surveying them with a curious expression – tinged with obvious undertones of impatience.

The girls made their way back to the counter.

Ava cleared her throat and then explained: 'The thing is, we found some money inside that book and we'd like to return it to the owner.' She made herself maintain eye contact with Mr Grimes, even though she was desperate to look away. 'A twenty-pound note.'

A crease appeared between the old man's bushy eyebrows, indicating that his inbuilt lie detector was tingling again. 'A twenty-pound note, you say?' he said with more than a hint of skepticism in his voice. 'Now why would someone leave money in a book?'

'Perhaps they used it as a bookmark and just forgot that it was there,' Libby suggested.

'That's an expensive bookmark,' Mr Grimes said.

'Maybe the previous owner is rich and twenty pounds is nothing to him or her,' Ava speculated.

'She isn't rich, I can assure you,' Mr Grimes said.

He knows the previous owner of the book! Ava thought. She once again looked at Libby, who looked back at her with wide eyes.

'At first, you told me that the book was having some strange effect on your friend, some dark influence,' Mr Grimes said. The crease between his eyebrows had now deepened to a full-blown scowl. 'And now you're telling me that you've found some money inside of it – twenty pounds, no less. That book has been in this shop for about six months, so I think someone – some browser – would have found it at some point, don't you?'

'The book doesn't exactly have the most appealing cover,' Ava said. 'And the browser would have had to open the book on exactly the right page to discover the note. And as for the book having a strange effect on our friend, we weren't lying about that. It's about dark magic, which isn't a good thing for anyone to be reading about, never mind someone of our age.'

'The key word here is "dark"' Libby said, nodding and smiling at Mr Grimes in a slightly condescending way.

'Yes, I know what the word means. But I still find it a bit of a stretch to think that no one found it in all that time.'

'Well, our friend did,' Ava said, 'and we can even show it to you if you like?' Out of the corner of her eye, she could see Libby giving her a sideways glance as if to say: can we?

'Why isn't your friend in here chasing up the previous owner herself?' Mr Grimes enquired in a snotty voice. 'Is she too afraid to come in? Why has she got you doing her legwork for her?'

'She had to go home early from school because she's ill,' Libby informed him.

'Ah, right, okay,' Mr Grimes said. 'So where is this twenty-pound note? Have you got it with you now? If so, hand it over and I'll make sure it gets back to the rightful owner.'

'We haven't got it with us,' Ava said. 'If you can give us the rightful owner's phone number or address then we'll make sure they get it.'

Mr Grimes rolled his old, bloodshot eyes. 'I am not in the habit of giving out addresses and phone numbers to people I don't know, I'm afraid. What you need to do is drop that note in here and, as I told you before, I'll make sure it gets back to the person it belongs to.'

'We'd rather give it back to her ourselves,' Libby said.

Mr Grimes drummed his stubby fingers impatiently on the counter. 'Look, I haven't got time for this,' he said. 'You want the recognition and the reward that goes with it, no doubt. So I'll ring her up now and see what she has to say. She is rather off the wall – rather kooky, as it were – so the idea of her using a twenty-pound note as a bookmark shouldn't surprise me too much, now I think about it.' He opened a drawer below the counter and began sifting through some paperwork. 'Drat! Where have I put my notepad with all the numbers in?' He slammed the drawer shut and then searched the shelves behind him. 'Ah – you see! This is what happens when you get old. You put things down and forget where you've put them. Ok, look, I'll just have to give you her address instead.' He scribbled it down on a piece of headed paper, folded it over, then held it out to Ava.

She went to take it from him, but then he withdrew his hand.

'Please tell me that I'm doing the right thing here?' he said, fixing both girls with searching looks. 'I'm not comfortable with giving out customer details (even if she is a good friend). If anything negative comes of this, then I'll … I'll ban you both from this shop for life. Are we clear on this?'

'Crystal,' Ava said, sticking out her chest and looking the old man dead in the eyes. 'And nothing negative will come of this, I can assure you. We're just going to give your friend back her money and …'

'Collect your reward,' Mr Grimes said, finishing her sentence.

'Yes,' Libby said, chirping in. 'Assuming that one is offered. And even if not, we'll still be grateful for just a thank you.'

'Oh, I bet you will,' Mr Grimes said in a sarcastic tone as he handed over the note to Ava.

'Right, well, thanks for that,' Libby as she made her way

towards the door with Ava.

The bell tinkled as they exited.

They moved down the street so that they were away from the shop.

Then Ava unfolded the note. 'Her name's Constance,' she said, 'and she lives at 53 Gravelpit Drive. Any idea where that is?'

'It's not far. About a five to ten-minute walk, depending on how fast we move.'

'Let's get going then. Quick steps …'

7.

Gravelpit Drive was a quiet road full of mostly semi-detached houses. Number 53 was the only double-fronted property. The place looked in need of renovation. Slates were missing from the roof, white paint peeling from the window frames. The garden was an overgrown jungle of weeds and knee-high grass.

Shielding her eyes against the sun, Libby pulled a face. 'Has he given us the right address?' she said. 'This place looks derelict.'

'We'll find out soon enough,' Ava said, 'when we knock on the door.'

'That's assuming that someone is in and they're willing to open it to a couple of strange kids.'

'Who you calling strange?' Ava said, fixing Libby with a playful sideways glare.

'It had to be the biggest, spookiest looking one of the lot, didn't it?' she said, looking up at the house again.

'Well, after you,' Ava said, gesturing her to go first.

'Oh, no,' Libby said, returning the gesture, 'I must insist ...'

Rolling her eyes, Ava led the way and pushed open the rickety gate.

As they made their way up the path, she caught a glimpse of movement in the large bay window to her left.

'I think I just saw someone watching us,' Libby said.

'Yep. Someone knows we're coming. Probably won't open the door now.'

The arched porch which led to the front door reminded Ava of a gaping mouth. A small sign on the wall warned that cold callers were not welcome.

Ava knocked ...

'Hmm, maybe they didn't hear you,' Libby said giving it a go herself with a good rap of her knuckles. 'There's no way that they're not hearing *that*.'

The girls waited. And waited ...

They saw no signs of movement behind the obscure glass in the top half of the door.

'Well, I think we can safely say that someone doesn't want to speak to us,' Libby said. 'Should we try knocking again? Or we could yell through the letterbox. What d'you think?'

'I think we'll have as much success with the letterbox as we're having with knocking. If whoever is in there is determined not to speak to us, then there isn't much we can do. Short of kicking the door in, I don't know what to suggest.'

Libby banged even harder, making the glass rattle in its frame.

'Careful!' Ava said. 'The last thing we need is to get arrested for criminal damage. Not sure how I'd explain *that* to my parents!'

They heard movement in the hallway. The distorted shape of a tall, dark figure appeared and called out: 'Who's there? Who's making that racket!'

Libby motioned for Ava to speak.

'Why me?' Ava whispered. 'Why can't you say something?'

Libby rolled her eyes and said, 'Err, we're sorry to disturb you, but we'd like to talk to you about something. We just need a few minutes of your time.'

'If you're cold callers then just bog off!' came the curt response. 'I don't need new windows and even if I did, I'm too broke to buy anything. And I know who I'm voting for at the next election, so you won't change my mind where that's concerned. Oh, and I'm not religious. You're not going to convert me to your beliefs, so don't waste my time or yours.'

'We're not cold callers,' Ava responded.

'I don't care who you are,' the woman said in an increasingly irritable tone, 'and I don't want to find out. Please go away and don't come back!'

Charming, Ava thought. She moved closer to the door so that she could be heard better, her face now only inches from the glass. 'We're looking for someone named Constance. It's about the book that she sold or gave to The Book Cove: the magical one – the one that she was probably keen to get rid of.'

Ava saw the woman advancing quickly toward her, so she retreated a few steps.

Bolts were thrown back, a key turned in the lock. The door swung in to reveal a weathered, tired-looking woman with long, scraggy brown hair. Other than her disheveled appearance, one of the first things Ava noticed was how tall she was: five feet ten at least. And she was thin, *painfully* thin. She looked as if she might not have eaten in weeks.

'Tell me that you haven't brought that book here!' the woman demanded to know. 'Tell me that you haven't brought that book anywhere near my house!'

'We haven't,' Libby assured her.

'It's with our friend,' Ava said. 'Are you Constance?'

The woman relaxed a little, her bony shoulders slumping. 'Yes, I am. How did you find me?' she said. 'How do you know my address?' But then she worked it out for herself. 'It was Bert from the shop, wasn't it? *He* sent you here.'

Ava nodded.

'Oooh! You wait till I see him …' Constance said, her voice laced with enough threat to suggest that Bert was in for an ear-bashing.

Ava said, 'Our friend has your book and …'

'Yes, so you told me,' Constance said, cutting her off. 'Well, whatever problems she's having with it are nothing to do with me. The moment she bought that book, it became hers, not mine. It became *her* problem, *not* mine. So what has she done that's got you worried? Which spell has the little witch performed that's got you pair so flustered? Has she shot a lightning bolt at someone? I remember when I first got that book; it was a spell that caught my eye. I couldn't wait to cast it.' She smiled wistfully, but then her expression darkened again as she focused on the girls. 'So come on then, which spell did your friend cast?'

'She made everyone at our school accident-prone,' Libby explained.

Constance looked surprised. 'Really? That's quite impressive. That's at the upper end of mid-level, I'd say. Your friend must be a powerful witch. But there is a downside to being able to do strong magic like that, which is probably another reason why you're here, no doubt. You've noticed the negative effects that it's had on her.'

'Negative effects!' Ava blurted. 'That's an understatement if ever I've heard one. Willow looked like she'd had the life drained out of her at the end of school today.'

'So why did she do all this?' Constance said. 'Why did she feel the need to make everyone at your school accident-prone?'

'She's being bullied,' Libby said.

'Ah, I see,' Constance said with an understanding nod. 'Well, whoever has chosen her as a target for bullying couldn't have made a worse choice, I can tell you. You need to have a word with your friend's oppressors and convince them to cease and desist. If your friend is making people have accidents now, imagine what she'll do to someone if the bullying continues.'

'Having "a word" isn't going to change anything,' Ava said. 'Ruth and Amy won't take any notice of us. And it's not like we can give them a warning about what'll happen to them if they don't back off. I can imagine how much they'll laugh at us if we tell them that Willow is a witch who can turn them into a pile of stinking poop. And then they'll tell the rest of the school, which will make things about twenty times worse.'

'Perhaps Ruth and Amy deserve what's coming to them,' Constance suggested with the ghost of a wicked smile touching her lips.

'Yes, they probably do,' Libby said. 'But we're more worried about Willow than anything else. You need to take that book back from her before she ends up seriously ill. We think that every time she does a spell, it takes something from her. Sucks the life out of her – drains her. Something like that. It's a book about dark magic, so it'll have a dark influence on her. No good can come from her having *that* book. And if anyone can convince her to give it up, it's you. Can you *please* help us?'

The look on Constance's face suggested not. 'Oh, I'm afraid I won't be going anywhere near that book ever again, thank you very much,' she said. 'You are very much right about it taking something from your friend. You only have to look at the state of me to see what the long-term effects will be. Have a guess how old I am?'

Ava estimated Constance to be in her sixties. She figured that she must be younger than she looked, however, so she plumped for mid-fifties. 'Err ... fifty-four?' she said.

Constance looked at Libby.

'I'd say ... late fifties,' she said.

'I'm thirty-eight in two weeks,' Constance said.

'*Thirty-eight!*' Libby blurted, her mouth dropping open in shock. 'Seriously?'

'Yes, seriously,' Constance replied.

'Wow!' Ava said under her breath.

'Yes, wow indeed,' Constance said. 'So you can see first-hand what'll happen to your friend if you don't get that book away from her. It won't be easy. She won't want to give it up, especially now she's had a taste for the amazing things she can do with it. And I wouldn't advise trying to steal it from her. She'll be liable to fly into a rage and ... well, who knows what she could do to you.'

'So our only option is to persuade her to get rid of it?' Ava said.

'That's right,' Constance confirmed.

'I don't like our chances,' Libby said.

'Me neither,' Ava moaned.

Constance said, 'The longer it's in her possession, the harder it will be to get it away from her.'

'And if we do manage to convince her to give it up,' Ava said, 'what do we do with it then? Destroy it? Burn it? Bury it in concrete? Or just hide it from her?'

'Don't do any of those things!' Constance warned her. 'The book cannot be destroyed and the consequences of attempting such things could be most dire. I tried burning it and narrowly escaped with my life. Hiding it won't help, either. When I owned the book, my bond with it was ridiculously strong, so I'd have found it easily if it'd been taken from me – no matter where it was. The best thing you can do is take it back to the shop and give it to Bert. He'll put it back on display and then someone should – fingers crossed! – eventually buy it.'

'Another witch, you mean?' Ava said.

'Yes,' Constance replied. 'Or a wizard.'

Wizards are a thing too! Ava thought.

'So what would happen if I bought the book?' Ava said. 'Would that solve the problem? I'm not magical, so it wouldn't affect me, right?'

'Non-magical people can't take ownership, I'm afraid,' Constance explained. 'Something would happen to prevent it. Either Bert will refuse to sell it to you – for whatever reason – or you'll suddenly feel compelled to not buy it (again, for whatever reason). It could never be that simple.'

'Bert told us that the book had been in his shop for about six months!' Libby exclaimed.

'Witches and wizards are not commonplace,' Constance said. 'The key thing is to be patient. Someone will be drawn to that book and they will buy it. The moment your friend made her purchase, I felt instant relief. The connection between me and that book was broken. Even if you do convince your friend to give the book back to the shop, she'll still be tempted to purchase it again. It will call out to her, so she needs to be strong. It won't be easy – but it can be done, because I've done it.'

'Don't you feel guilty for palming it off on someone else?' Libby said. 'Willow is a school kid, like us. That makes it even worse.'

'Of course I feel guilty!' Constance snapped at her. 'But you haven't had to live through what I have, so you don't know what it's like. Every spell I've done has drained me, taken something from me. I mean, look at me! Look at what it's done to me. And you want me to go near that book again! Not a chance. Not for anybody or anyone. And especially not for someone I don't even know!'

'It shouldn't matter whether you know them or not,' Ava said. 'If I was in your position, I'd help. I'd feel awful lumbering that burden on someone else.'

'And so would I,' Libby added.

'Yes, well, I'm not you pair, am I!' Constance said, glaring at them.

'Where did you get the book from?' Libby asked her. 'Do you know who owned it before you? Maybe they can help us.'

'I found it in a bookstore down south,' Constance explained. 'When I bought it, the woman behind the counter told me that it'd been in the shop for some time, so she was glad to be rid of it. Sometime later – after I realized how dangerous the book was – I went back and quizzed her about it. She couldn't remember how she'd come by it, so that was the end of that.' Constance checked the time on her watch and sighed. 'Look, I've told you everything I know about that book and said everything that needs to be said. So with that in mind, can you please remove yourself from my property so I can sit down? You showing up here unannounced has taken all the energy out of me. It doesn't take much these days, as you can imagine.'

Constance went to close the door, so Ava put her foot in the way.

'Our business is concluded,' Constance said with an underlying tone of threat. 'Please go away!'

Ava kept her foot in place for a few more seconds and then removed it.

'Just one last thing,' Libby said to Constance. 'Will Willow be able to ride a broomstick?'

She rolled her eyes and said, 'Yes, of course.' Then she slammed the door shut hard enough to rattle the glass in its frame.

'Charming,' Libby said. She noticed that Ava was giving her a funny look. 'What? Sorry, but I had to ask. I was *dying* to know.'

Ava banged on the glass with her fist. '*Hey!* You can't just leave us here like this!' she raged. 'You have to help our friend! You *have* to! Hey!' She banged again. Louder this time. '*HEYYYY!*'

'Stop doing that!' Libby said, putting a hand on her shoulder. 'She'll call the police if you keep on.'

'That's exactly what I'm going to do if you don't go away!' Constance said from down the hallway. 'I'll give you one minute to get off my property!'

Ava shrugged Libby's hand away and then kicked the door.

'Calling the police may not be the worst thing she can do to us,' Libby said in a low voice. 'Might be worth remembering that she's a witch, yeah?'

Witch or not, Ava was tempted to give the door another kick anyway. 'You're a sad excuse for a human being!' she said through the glass. 'And I hope that Karma comes to get you!'

'It already has,' Constance replied.

Libby took Ava by the arm. 'Come on,' she said, attempting to shepherd her away, 'let's get out of here before Karma comes for us.'

Reluctantly, Ava allowed herself to be led down the path and through the gate. 'Well, that went well,' she said, kicking out at nothing but air. 'Her only advice is to get that book away from Willow. Like we hadn't already figured that out anyway.'

'At least we've seen what it'll do to Willow if she keeps it. We could have done with her being with us so she could see the state of that woman. Hey, maybe we should bring her here when she's well enough. Seeing that woman up close and personal could shock her into taking it back to the shop. What do you think?'

'A moment ago you were worried that the woman might turn us into toads or something – and now you want to go knocking on her door again. I doubt she'd answer anyway. And even if she did, she'd take one look at us and slam the door in our faces.'

'Who said anything about knocking on the door?' Libby looked around, casing out the street. She pointed to a house across the road. 'That place is up for sale and it doesn't look as if anybody's living there. We could hide in the bushes at the front of the garden and Willow could get a look at her that way. That woman will leave the house at some point or look out of the window. I'm pretty sure my dad has some binoculars somewhere from when he used to do bird watching. Willow could get a close-up look at Constance without having to go anywhere near her.'

'What if we get caught? How are we going to explain being in a bush?'

'We'll just ... bring a ball with us and say that we lost it in there.'

'Sounds plausible. Unless it's Constance who catches us, of course. I don't think that lie will fly with her.'

'Ah, well, that's when we go to plan B, which involves legging it away as quickly as possible. That woman doesn't know who we are or where we live – and she's in no state to catch us.'

'No, she won't be able to catch us – but she could use magic against us. She could probably freeze us with a few words and a death stare.'

'Best not get caught then,' Libby said, offering a shrug.

Ava looked back at the kooky house and scowled. 'I still

can't believe that she won't help us,' she said. The scowl softened a little as she turned toward her friend. 'And I still can't believe you asked her whether Willow will be able to ride a broomstick. I mean, seriously? What a thing to ask at a time like this!'

Libby offered another shrug, along with an apologetic smile. 'I'm sorry. But as I said, I just couldn't resist. I had to know one way or another. I can't think of anything cooler than being able to ride a broomstick and Willow will be able to do that.'

'Oh well,' Ava said, 'at least we now know for certain what's causing Willow to be ill.'

She saw one of the downstairs curtains twitch. A flash of shadowy movement …

'Did you just see that?' she said.

'Yep. I think it might be a good idea if we distanced ourselves from here, or we could end up getting the death stare (if that's a thing).'

The girls began walking.

'So what are we going to do next?' Libby said. 'We need to talk to Willow but we can't because she's ill. If we visit her house, her parents will just send us away.'

'We'll just have to be patient. Give it a few days, at least. If she isn't back at school by Friday, then we'll go knocking. It's frustrating because I want to do something about it now, but it's the only option we've got. Agreed?'

'Yeah – agreed.'

8.

Thursday began with an impromptu assembly. A concerned Mrs Fernsby addressed the students about the accidents that'd taken place the previous day. Her voice echoed around the hall as she detailed the injuries that had been sustained.

'In all my years at this school, I have never known such a bizarre collection of incidents to take place in such a short space of time,' she said. 'Let us hope that yesterday was just a one-off and that we can now go back to the normality of the occasional mishap (which is to be expected). I've assured the concerned parents who've contacted me that you will all be extra cautious today while going about your business ...'

Ava tuned herself out of the rest of the headmistress's speech by taking an interest in everything apart from the one thing she was supposed to be focusing her attention on. And Libby was just as distracted as well, sporting a wistful expression which suggested that she was somewhere more interesting than school (in her imagination, at least).

Throughout the morning, Ava and Libby got sick of overhearing other students talking about the accidents. One boy speculated about the odds of so many unfortunate things taking place in a matter of hours and he suggested that supernatural forces could have been at work. His talk of ghosts or specters was met with derision from his fellow students.

Getting through the rest of the day without having any

run-ins with the bullies proved to be challenging for the girls. Ruth and Amy seemed to be determined to make their lives hell with every opportunity they got. Standing up to them didn't do any good. In fact, it had the opposite effect – it added tinder to the fire. The threat of detentions from Mrs Fernsby wasn't deterring them in the slightest. The bullies were eager for a fight, but Ava and Libby were smart enough to know that they would probably come off second-best if it came to fisticuffs.

'All of that hassle is waiting for Willow when she comes back,' Libby said to Ava as they walked home. 'And it'll be even worse for her. Are we still on for tomorrow? Are we still going to her house if she's not back at school?'

'Yup. I'm still up for it if you are.'

Libby said. 'We can go after my detention.'

'Oh, I forgot about that!'

'Miss Becker hasn't. She reminded me earlier when she saw me in the corridor.'

'Do your parents know about it?'

'Yes, she contacted them. My mum and dad were not impressed. But I explained the situation to them and they chilled a bit then. They advised me to steer clear of Ruth and Amy. And they told me to keep them informed of any other nasty incidents that happen.'

'Let's just hope you don't have to inform them of anything else.'

A roll of her eyes and a shake of her head communicated Libby's thoughts on the chances of that being the case.

9.

Friday ...

Ava and Libby had heard of Welbeck Street but they'd never been anywhere near it, or the surrounding area, before. And with good reason. Their parents had told them to steer clear as it was on the "rough side" of town. As the girls rounded the corner onto the street, a group of hoodie-wearing boys called out to them, asking them where they were going.

'Just keep your head down and ignore them,' Ava advised as they both did just that.

'Hey!' one of the boys shouted. 'Don't you know it's rude to ignore people!'

The girls kept walking. Ava glanced over her shoulder to see if they were being followed and was alarmed to see that they were. Libby noticed too and quickened her pace.

'It's number 52,' Ava said, 'just up here on the right.'

Another glance over her shoulder made her break into a jog. Libby followed suit and they soon arrived at the house: a grotty-looking 1970s semi-detached with a rusty old Vauxhall Cavalier on the driveway. They hurried through the gate, down the path, then waited by the front door.

'Do you think they'll try and get us here?' Libby said. 'Or will they just walk past and hurl more abuse?'

'I don't want to hang around to find out,' Ava said, pressing the doorbell.

The door opened just as the boys came into view and the girls resisted the temptation to turn and look at them again.

'Can I help you?' a gruff voice said.

The girls were greeted by a huge man. Very overweight, his flabby belly hung from beneath his t-shirt in an unflattering way. He had dark, greasy hair and a stubbly chin that he was scratching as he regarded the girls with a curious expression. Both girls were slightly taken aback by the sheer size of the man, who almost filled the doorway. Ava assumed that he must be Willow's father.

'Can I help you?' he asked again, this time with a little more urgency in his voice.

'We're friends of Willow's from school and we've come to see if she's feeling better,' Libby said.

'We've been worried about her,' Ava added.

'She is feeling better,' the man said, 'but I'm not sure if she's well enough to see anyone yet. If you could come back Sunday, she might be up to it then.'

'We'd only take up five minutes of her time,' Ava said. 'Not even that really. We just want to say hello and she'll probably be glad to see us.'

'I'm sure she would,' the man said, 'but ...'

'Dad, can you just let them in, please!' Willow called down from the top of the stairs. 'I want to see them.'

'Are you sure you're up to it, love?' he asked her.

'What the ruddy hell is all that noise!' someone else said.

A short, wiry woman burst into view and glared at the visitors. 'Who the 'eck are you and why are you making so much of a racket?' she said. 'I'm trying to watch a TV program and all I can hear is voices, voices, voices! So whaddaya want?'

'They're friends of Willow's,' the dad explained. 'Here to see if she's okay.'

'Not yet, she isn't,' the woman said irritably. 'You'll have to come back another day. Next week, maybe, when she's had more time to recover.'

Willow checked behind her to see if the hoodie-wearing thugs were still hanging around, but they were nowhere to be seen. If she and Libby were about to be sent away then the last thing they needed was to run into that lot again.

'Mum, I'm well enough to see them,' Willow called down. 'Can you please just send them up.'

Willow's dad stepped back and gestured for the girls to enter. Even though he'd moved to one side to make way, the girls still struggled to get past him. They had to flatten themselves against the open door while a mixture of BO and bad breath assaulted their senses. Ava felt like cringing but managed a forced smile instead.

Willow motioned for her friends to come up and they didn't waste a second in doing so.

'Make it a short visit because the takeaway will be here soon!' Willow's mum hollered after them. 'And don't go making loads of noise up there either, otherwise I'll get ticked off!'

'Okay, Mum,' Willow said as she shepherded her friends across the landing and into a small, boxlike bedroom.

Willow closed the door and looked at her friends.

'Well, you look a lot better,' Libby said to her. 'You've got some color back in your cheeks.'

'I feel a lot better. Still haven't got much of an appetite but I'm sure it'll come back.'

Ava admired some posters on the wall: one featuring Wham and another showcasing the Queen of Pop at her glitzy best. 'I like your taste in music,' she said. 'Have you got Madonna's latest album?'

Willow shook her head. 'I could get it for my birthday,' she said. 'It's next month, so I don't have long to wait.'

'Yeah, definitely get it,' Libby agreed. 'There are some really good songs on there.'

'I will,' Ava assured her.

An awkward silence followed, which was broken by Willow: 'So,' she said, 'what can I do for you pair then? You've come to see if I'm getting better, but I can see from the looks on your faces that there's something else.'

Libby said, 'It's about the …'

'Book,' Willow said, finishing the sentence for her. 'Yeah?'

'Yeah,' Ava said. 'We've done some investigating and it's not good news.'

Willow slouched into a reclining chair in the corner and gestured for the girls to get comfy on her bed, which they did.

'So what investigating have you done?' Willow enquired. 'What have you found out?'

Ava explained how she and Libby had gone to the

bookshop to question Mr Grimes. 'He gave us the address of the woman who owned the book before you,' Ava said.

'Her name is Constance and we paid her a visit,' Libby said.

'You did?' Willow said. Her tone and manner suggested a mixture of intrigue and concern. 'And what did she have to say about it then?'

'She told us that you need to get rid of that book,' Willow said.

'Ta-da!' Willow exclaimed. 'Now why did I know you were going to say *that*!'

'Just listen to us, will you?' Ava said, edging forward and fixing her with a serious stare. 'When the woman answered the door, we thought that she was old: maybe in her sixties or something. But she told us that she was only half that age. Doing magic with that book has taken something out of her. Honestly, you should have seen the state of her. I've seen zombies with more life than that woman. And that's what'll happen to you if you continue using that book.'

'Maybe she used it too much,' Willow speculated.

'She probably did,' Libby said. 'But that's what you'll do if you insist on keeping it.'

'I haven't "insisted" on anything,' Willow said. 'I've already told you what I'm going to do where the book is concerned. If I feel like it's having too much of a negative effect on me, I'll get rid. There's one thing you need to understand, though. That book is the coolest thing that's ever happened to me and so I'm not going to give up on it easily. And don't look at me like that, you pair. Just because I've said that I won't give up on it easily doesn't mean that I won't be able to. The woman who owned it before me managed to do it, so that's got to be a good thing, right?'

'It only ceased to be hers and be an influence on her when you bought it. And that's the only way you'll ever be rid of it is by taking it back to the shop and someone else buying it. The book can't be destroyed. Constance tried to burn it and narrowly escaped with her life.'

'Narrowly escaped with her life?' Willow said. 'What, did the book attack her or something?'

'She didn't say,' Libby said, 'but the bottom line is that you need to say goodbye to that book – and the quicker, the better.'

Willow took a few seconds to process this new information, then assured her friends that she would be very careful where the book was concerned. 'And when another person buys the book from the shop,' she said, 'would I be right in thinking that I'll be passing the problem on to someone else?'

'Yes,' Ava confirmed. 'I know it sounds awful, but there is no other way. We tried to convince Constance to help us but she wouldn't. The only way she could have helped us is by buying back the book, which – surprise, surprise – she isn't prepared to do.'

'I don't like the idea of lumbering someone else with my problem,' Willow said.

'We don't like it either,' Libby said, 'but it's the only way.'

'How can you know for sure?' Willow said.

Libby looked at Ava, who shrugged.

'Just because this Constance told you that it's the only way doesn't necessarily mean that it's the case,' Willow said.

'Maybe there is and maybe there isn't,' Ava said, 'but you parting company with that book can be the only acceptable end result. Unless you want to end up like Constance. Libby suggested taking you to visit her, just so you can see her with your own eyes.'

'I don't need to see her,' Willow said with an edge of irritation creeping into her voice. 'I get everything you're saying and I can imagine what a state she is. Look, I still don't feel that great but I could be well enough to go to school on Monday if I can rest. My dad took me to see the doctor and that was his advice: get plenty of rest.'

'I'm guessing that the doctor didn't have a clue what's wrong with you,' Libby said.

'That's right,' Willow confirmed. 'I had blood tests done and all sorts. The only thing he could suggest was that school could be troubling me, the stressful environment bringing on the sickness. Well, he wasn't wrong about it troubling me – but not in the way that he thinks. And speaking of those idiots, have they been giving you any problems while I've been off?'

'They're always giving us problems,' Ava said, 'but, yeah, they've been even worse than normal now that you're not there.'

Willow shifted uneasily in her seat. 'So I can expect more

of the same when I do return, then, yeah?' Willow said.

'Almost certainly,' Libby said.

'I think you can cut out the almost,' Ava said.

Willow's expression hardened. 'Something needs to be done about those pair,' she said, 'otherwise nothing will change.'

Ava exchanged a concerned look with Libby.

This did not go unnoticed by Willow, who was quick to assure them that she wouldn't do anything silly. 'Although I can't deny it,' she said, 'the temptation to make them just disappear is *really* pulling at me.'

'Please don't do anything like that,' Ava begged her. 'Promise me that you won't use magic on either of them.'

'I won't use magic,' Willow said.

'That wasn't a promise,' Libby noted.

'Okay,' Willow said, rolling her eyes. 'I *promise* that I won't use magic against the idiots.'

Ava relaxed a little at hearing this.

'So how did your detention go?' Willow asked Libby.

'Oh, it was very exciting. Best hour of fun I've had in ages.' Libby rolled her eyes to show that she was joking. 'Can't wait to get another one.'

Willow managed a giggle in response

'So, have you done any magic while you've been at home?' Ava asked her. 'Has temptation got the better of you? Where's the book? Do you need to have it with you to perform spells?'

Willow opened her mouth, paused before speaking, and

then admitted to having done a few basic spells. 'I've mostly been levitating stuff because that's about as easy as it gets when it comes to spells. The book is hidden where my parents, or anyone else, won't find it. And, no, I don't need to have it with me.'

'Is it wise to do magic while you're still ill, though?' Libby said.

'Probably not,' Willow admitted. 'But I just couldn't resist having a try.'

Ava thought: *and that, in a nutshell, is going to be the problem …*

The sound of heavy footfalls on the stairs made the girls look toward the door.

A few seconds later, Willow's dad opened it partly and stuck his hulking head through the gap. 'The food will be here in a few minutes,' he announced, 'so if you could begin wrapping things up, then that would be great, ta muchly.' He gave everyone a nod and then closed the door. The heavy footfalls decreased in loudness as he made his way back downstairs.

'I know he looks scary,' Willow said, 'but he's a big teddy bear really. It's my mum who's the dragon, as you've probably noticed.'

'Your mum seems … okay,' Ava said, lying.

Bedsprings pinged as she got up, went to the window, then looked left and right, casing out the street.

'Are they still around?' Libby said. 'Please tell me that they aren't?'

'Is who still around?' Willow said, concerned.

Ava explained about the gang of hoodies: about how they'd followed her and Libby down the street. 'They disappeared when we got to your house,' Ava said. 'They disappeared when your dad answered the door.'

'That doesn't surprise me,' Willow said. 'I think they're a bit scared of him. I can't possibly think why,' she added with a giggle. She joined Ava by the window and cased out the street for herself. 'Well, I can't see them, but that doesn't mean that they're not around, which they probably are.' She pointed to the left. 'They usually hang around the corner down there, so I'd go the other way when you leave.'

'Yeah, that's where they were when we arrived,' Libby said.

'Uh, I think your takeaway's here,' Ava said. 'A guy on a moped has just pulled up and he's getting a brown bag out of a container on the back.'

Willow beamed: 'I'm looking forward to this! I love Chinese food.'

'Nothing wrong with your appetite then?' Libby said.

'As I said, I still don't feel one hundred per cent,' Willow said, 'but there's no way I was turning down a takeaway. We don't get that many. This is a rare treat.'

Her mum called up the stairs: 'Willow! The food's arrived! It's time for your friends to leave!'

'Okay, we'll leave you to it,' Ava said, making for the door.

'Oooh! Just one last thing before we go,' Libby said, grinning excitedly at Willow. 'I asked Constance if you'd be able to ride a broomstick and she said yes.'

Willow's face brightened. 'Seriously?' she said. 'And where would I get one of those? Would it just be a normal one from a utility store? Or would it have to be an enchanted one or something?'

Libby shrugged. 'I dunno; I didn't think to ask her about that. Is there anything in your book about broomsticks?'

'Not that I've noticed,' Willow replied. 'I'll take another look this evening. But it is a book about spells, so I don't think it'll cover something like that.'

Her mum called up the stairs again, making the girls jump: '*Willllow! Get your backside down here NOW! Your food'll get cold!*'

'Right, sorry you pair,' Willow said, bundling her friends through the doorway, 'but it's time to go. If you think my mum's angry now, you don't want to see her when her sweet and sour balls have gone cold.'

'Sweet and sour what?' Libby said.

Willow escorted them up the driveway, then checked left and right. 'The coast appears to be clear,' she declared. 'No hoodlums in sight.'

'Do you think we'll be okay to go back the way we came?' Ava asked her.

'I'd go the other way,' Willow advised, 'Just to be on the safe side.' She nodded toward the opposite end of the street. 'Right, I better get inside before Mum appears at the door and embarrasses me,' she said, backing away toward the house. 'And hopefully I'll see you at school on Monday.'

Ava and Libby gave her a smile and a wave and watched her as she disappeared inside.

'Damn!' Ava said, 'I should have reminded her not to do any more magic.

'Well, she knows what effect it'll have on her.'

'Somehow, I don't think that'll stop her. Do you?'

'She's already admitted to levitating stuff, so probably not.'

'Did you have to say about her being able to ride a broomstick?'

'How could I *not* tell her something like that?'

'The idea is for us to discourage her from doing magic because of what effect it'll have on her.'

'I know. But she did look a lot better, though; even with doing those other little spells. I promise I won't say anything else to encourage her.'

The first shades of darkness were beginning to edge across the land. A slight wind picked up, rustling the branches of nearby trees as Ava looked up at the sky and noted some dark clouds coming in from the east.

'I think it's going to rain soon,' she said, 'so let's not hang about. I wouldn't want to be around here after dark; it's intimidating enough during the day.'

As they began walking, Libby glanced over her shoulder and visibly stiffened. 'Err, how fast are you at running?' she said with obvious fear in her voice.

Ava didn't need to look to know what she would see, but she did it anyway. 'Okay great, just what we need,' she said, quickening her pace in unison with Libby. 'When we get around the corner we leg it, yeah?'

'Yep. Where's that magical broomstick when we need it?'

'Forget the broomstick. I'd turn them into leeches if I could.'

'Is that book having a bad influence on you too, Ava?'

'No, I'm pretty sure I'd want to do something like that to them whether there was an evil book around or not.'

Ava noticed that the thugs were gaining ground on them. She quickened her pace again and so did Libby.

'This is my top speed where walking is concerned!' Libby stated. 'We should have gone back to Willow's house when we had the chance.'

'What, and risk disturbing the family takeaway. Honestly, I'm more afraid of Willow's mum than I am of the hoodie-wearing turds.'

'Oi! Wait up!' one of them yelled. 'What are you running away for? We just wanna talk to yeh!'

'Yeah, and I'm sure it'll be a *really* pleasant conversation,' Libby said.

She and Ava rounded the corner. They were both about to begin sprinting – but instead they stopped dead in their tracks because two boys were blocking their way: hoodie-wearing thugs with their arms folded across their chests.

'What's the rush?' the tall one on the left said.

'Got somewhere you need to be, have yeh?' the other one said.

'Yes we have,' Libby said in a surprisingly amiable tone, 'so if you could just move out of the way, we'd be very grateful, ta.'

'That's not going to happen,' the tall one said.

Ava and Libby heard footsteps behind them and turned to see that the other hoodies had caught up with them. In all, it was now eight vs two. Ava did not like the odds. She did *not* like them at all.

'Give us your money and we'll let yeh go on yeh way,' one of the boys from the larger group said.

'I don't have any on me,' Ava said, turning out her pockets. She looked at Libby, who shook her head.

'I haven't got any on me either,' she said.

'Turn out your pockets,' the boy ordered her.

She did as she was told.

'That's a nice watch you're wearing,' one of the boys noticed.

Libby placed her hand protectively over it. 'It was a gift from my grandma,' she said sternly. 'She gave it to me just before she died, so there's no way you're taking this from me.' Her eyes narrowed and she pressed her lips tightly together as a show of determination.

'One way or another, you're going to give us that watch,' the same boy said, 'so we can either do this the physical or non-physical way. Your choice!'

'Why don't you just get lost!' Ava said, moving closer to her friend. 'How does that sound?'

'It sounds like you just chose the physical way,' the boy said as he balled his hands into fists and began to move forward. 'This is your last chance. Hand it over!'

'I think now might be a good time to leg it,' Libby said to Ava through the side of her mouth.

'Where to?' Ava said. 'They've got us surrounded!'

'We can't just stand here!' Libby said. 'I can't give this to them,' she added, once again covering the watch protectively with her hand. 'I just *can't!*'

But Ava could see that the resolve on her face was beginning to dissolve.

The boy was nearly close enough to strike out at the girls now, so they took a compensatory step back for every one of his.

The hoodies behind them beckoned them to continue their retreat.

'That's it – keep coming this way!' the tall one said, reaching into his pocket and teasing to pull something out. 'I've got a little something for you!'

Ava caught a glimpse of a metal glint and then Libby let out a gasp of fear.

'Okay, *okay!*' Libby said, fumbling to unstrap her watch. 'You can have it! You can *have it!*'

She was just about to hand it over to the boy who'd been advancing on them when, all of a sudden, his jeans became unbuckled and fell to the ground. A moment of silence followed as the girls looked at him and he looked at them, open-mouthed.

'What the hell!' he said, snatching them quickly back up and fumbling to secure them.

A few of the other hoodies let out giggles.

'Shur up!' the fumbling boy said as he secured his top button. He turned his attention back to Libby. 'And, you, give me that watch! Give it to me *NOW!*'

Libby was about to do just that ...

But then the boy's jeans fell down again. And this time it wasn't just a few of his friends who giggled – they all burst out laughing, some of them doubling over in stitches.

'SHUR UP!' the boy yelled. He tried to pull his jeans up but couldn't. They appeared to be stuck around his ankles. 'What the *actual* hell!' No matter how hard he tugged, he just couldn't get them to move. 'STOP LAUGHING! SHUR UP AND HELP ME!'

And then they all did shut up – as the sound of police sirens began warbling nearby. There was a moment of silence as all the hoodies exchanged worried glances. The first one bolted – then the next. And then that was it, they were all running away, some in one direction and some in the other. This just left the jeans boy, who was still trying frantically to pull up his leg-wear.

'I'd get moving if I were you,' Ava advised him. 'The police will be here any minute and this will get even more embarrassing for you.'

'You should try hopping,' Libby said through fits of giggles. 'That's what I'd do.'

The boy snarled at her and then did just that. He began hopping away, back in the direction of Willow's house.

And then it was Ava's turn to break out into fits of giggles.

'Oh that's just about the funniest thing I've ever seen in my life!' she said, laughing so hard that she had to clutch at her guts. 'What is going on? What in the *actual* heck is going on!'

'Willow!' Libby said, her expression brightening as she looked toward the nearest end of the street.

Ava followed her gaze and noticed that Willow was leaning against a lamppost. She was holding her magic book and sporting a very pleased-with-herself grin.

Ava and Libby made their way over to her and thanked her for the intervention.

'How did you know that we needed help?' Libby asked Willow.

'After you left, I got this weird sensation that something wasn't right,' she explained, 'so I went back to my bedroom and looked out of my window. And that's when I saw that lot skulking after you down the road. I know what you're going to say: that I shouldn't have done any more magic when I'm still recovering from being ill. But I don't regret doing it — even if I do feel like crap now. I couldn't hear what was being said from here, but it looked like they were trying to get you to hand over your watch, Libby. Am I right?'

'That's right,' she confirmed. 'It's the only thing of value that we've got on us. It belonged to my grandma, though, so I was adamant that they wouldn't take it from me.'

'Until one of them was about to pull a knife on us,' Ava said.

Libby said, 'When I saw that flash of metal, I knew I had to hand it over. It's not worth risking our lives for a watch —

even if it means a lot to me.' She smiled down at it, then looked down the street and smiled again. 'Ha-ha! How long are those jeans going to stay around his ankles like that?'

'I have no idea,' Willow said, sporting a wide, toothy grin.

'Did you see the look on his face?' Libby said.

'Did you see the look on *all* of their faces?' Ava added.

'Well, they should think themselves lucky,' Willow said, 'because I could have done far worse than that. They got off quite lightly, I'd say.'

'Very lightly,' Libby agreed. She glanced around in different directions, seemingly confused. 'Those siren sounds aren't getting any closer or louder …' And then she realized. 'Ah, you didn't really call the police, did you?' she said to Willow. 'The sirens are just a spell, aren't they?'

'Yep,' she confirmed proudly. She ended the warbling with a click of her fingers.

Ava nodded towards Jeans Boy, who'd only made it halfway down the road so far. 'He might come back if he thinks the police aren't coming,' she said. 'And his friends: they might come back too.'

'I can start the sirens again,' Willow said. 'It's not a problem – easily done.'

'No, you better not,' Ava said, 'because that would mean you doing magic again and you're not meant to be doing any while you're recovering.' *And we don't really want you doing any at all,* she thought, *what with your magic book being an evil one and all that.* She cast a troubled glance at the book, which Willow was clutching tightly in her hands.

'I think we may have already attracted enough unwanted attention,' Libby said, nodding at a nearby house. 'That old woman with her face between the curtains looks like the type who'd call the police at the first sign of trouble, so we could hear some real sirens soon if we hang around here long enough.'

'She's not the only curtain twitcher either,' Ava added. 'I noticed people watching us while we were having trouble with those boys. They'll have seen everything and heard the sirens, so they'll be expecting the police to turn up. And when they don't …'

'Okay, look, I need to get back inside anyway,' Willow said. 'If my mum notices that I'm out here and letting my takeaway go cold, she won't be happy. Although I don't feel too hungry now, to be honest. Casting those spells has dampened my appetite.'

The girls let out a collective giggle as Jeans Boy once again took a tumble.

'Do you know who he is?' Libby asked Willow. 'Do you know any of his gang?'

'No, I don't think any of them live around here,' she responded. 'They showed up about two weeks ago and have been hanging around, on and off, ever since. They probably relocate to different areas all the time, looking for easy targets.'

'And we were the easy targets here,' Ava said. She wasn't comfortable with the idea of being thought of as an easy target. Two girls at school also thought that she was an easy target – and they needed sorting out too.

'But they saw us go to your house,' Libby said to Willow. 'Aren't you worried that they might come back for revenge? Did any of them notice you as they were fleeing?'

'I'm pretty sure they didn't,' she replied. 'They were too busy being scared and fleeing. And, besides, like I said before, they're scared of my dad. They won't come anywhere near our house. And if they do …' she held up her book and smiled, 'I can always remind them what happens when you cause trouble around here.'

'That would have to be a last resort,' Libby said.

'It would be,' Willow assured her.

Ava noted the color was beginning to drain from Willow's face and that she was slurring her words a little. *You're becoming addicted to it*, she thought, eyeing the book through narrowed eyes. *You just can't help yourself*.

'Erm, you know that old woman who was watching us from through her curtains,' Libby said, gesturing discreetly toward the house. 'Well, she's now got a phone pressed to her ear and I'm guessing that she isn't calling for a takeaway. We really should move before the real police turn up.'

'Right, I'm going to get back inside before Mum comes outside and starts shouting in the street,' Willow said, backing away toward her house. 'You should be okay to go back the way you came now. I'm sure it'll be safe.' She raised a hand, then turned away and broke into a kind of skipping jog.

Ava and Libby watched as she disappeared down her

driveway.

'She really shouldn't be moving around like that when she still isn't well,' Libby said as she and Ava got walking.

'And she shouldn't be doing magic either. Although I don't like to think of what might have happened if she hadn't. Did you see how pale she looked? I know she was smiling and joking and that, but she still isn't well. And every spell she does will take something out of her, drain her like a vampire, little by little, bit by bit. We have to get that book away from her – but how?'

'The only thing we need to concentrate on at the moment is distancing ourselves from here. I'm sure something will occur to us where Libby is concerned. Where there's a will there's a way and all that. There's a solution for every problem if you're determined enough, my mum has always told me – and we're going to find a way around this problem.'

'I wish I shared your optimism.'

They looked at Willow's house as they passed and didn't notice movement behind any of the windows.

Jeans Boy had finally managed to make his way to the end of the road. The girls watched in amusement as he reached down and was able to yank up his jeans. He disappeared out of sight, moving considerably quicker than he'd been able to before.

'I guess the spell wore off,' Libby said with a chuckle.

'Let's just hope that's the last time we ever see him or any of his idiot mates. Come on, let's get moving. I forgot to tell my mum that I'd be home late, so she'll probably be worrying now.'

'Yeah, I'll probably get an earful as well'

'Best get a move on then,' Ava said, jogging ahead. 'I'll race you!'

Libby took off after her with a determined grin on her face.

10.

Ava's mum did indeed give her a roasting when she arrived home. She interrogated her with the questions Ava expected: Where have you been? What sort of time do you call this? Do you have any idea how worried me and your father have been? Ava made up some wishy-washy excuse about stopping off at the park, which her mother accepted whilst scrutinizing her through narrowed eyes. And then, of course, came the extra telling off for not keeping her mother informed about what she was doing. With her ears still ringing from the harsh words, Ava skulked off to her bedroom for most of the evening.

11.

Throughout the weekend, Ava racked her brain, trying to think of a way to get Willow to part with her book. But she couldn't think of a single way to do it without things ending badly. When she next saw Libby again, on Sunday, she was just as clueless as well. They were at the park, going back and forth on the swings. It was a windy day. Gusts were buffeting them from the east, clouds skudding across the sky as if they were racing each other.

'Let's just see what Willow has to say about it when we next see her,' Libby said, 'which'll hopefully be tomorrow.'

'I don't think we'll see her tomorrow,' Ava said. 'Not after those extra spells she did. It's bound to have taken something out of her. Depends on how easy they were to perform, I suppose. When she does come back, we need to keep her away from Ruth, because that situation is only going to get worse. Ruth is giving us a hard time, so imagine what she'll be like with Willow.'

'Agreed,' Libby said, bringing herself to a skidding halt.

Ava put her head back and relished the cool wind on her cheeks. She watched the clouds fly by overhead, mulling things over. Then she also brought herself to a halt.

'We just need to stick to doing what we said we were going to do,' Libby said, 'which involves being patient. But not for too long, hopefully. When Willow returns to school, we'll convince her to get rid of the book. We'll keep bugging her about it until she's so sick of listening to us that she'll do anything to shut us up.'

'Anything?' Ava said, giving her a sharp sideways look. 'As long as it doesn't involve magic, though, right?'

'She wouldn't do anything to harm us,' Libby said. 'I'd bet a big wad of money on it.'

'You don't look as sure as you sound,' Ava noted.

'It's a shame that she doesn't need a wand to do magic,' Libby said, sidestepping her friend's observation. 'We could have just snatched it away from her. Problem solved.'

'It could never be that easy.'

'Of course it couldn't. But, yeah, it is a shame that she doesn't need a wand.'

12.

Monday and Tuesday passed without Willow putting in an appearance at school.

'If she doesn't show up tomorrow,' Libby said as they were making their way slowly to the dinner hall, 'do you think we should pay her another visit? We could tell our parents that there's an after-school activity we want to attend. That way, we won't get an earful when we get home late.'

'I like your forward-thinking, but what sort of after-school activity are we talking about here? Chess? Pottery? Football?'

'Oh hell no! And a double hell-no for chess. It needs to be something believable. Something that they might think that we *actually* want to go to.'

'Pottery does sound kind of interesting.'

'You'd be interested in that? Seriously?'

'Unless you can think of something better?'

'I can. There's a cookery club I've considered going to it. I love the idea of baking cakes and stuff, so that'll wash with my parents. What do you reckon?'

'Well, it's a lot more believable than the idea of us rocking up at chess club. Hmmm ... yeah, I think my parents will go for it too.'

'Rights, that's it – we're decided. If she doesn't show up here by Wednesday we pay her a visit, yeah? Hopefully we won't interrupt a takeaway and hopefully Willow's mum won't be there.'

'Hopefully we won't see those thugs again.'

'Oh, I don't think we'll see them again – not after what happened to them last time.'

The girls exchanged an amused look as they pushed through some double doors.

'And I don't think we'll be interrupting any takeaways,' Ava said. 'That was a rare treat they were having, remember? I still feel guilty for interrupting them. And I felt guilty when I got home and compared the house and area I'm living in to where Willow is living.'

'Yeah, I felt guilty as we were making our way through her house. But there isn't anything we can do about that. All we can do is be a good friend to her and be there for her when she needs us. And hope that she doesn't blow us up if we naff her off.'

The girls exchanged another amused look as they went through another set of doors and entered the hall. They joined the queue to get their food, snatching up a tray each. The girls raised their voices as they spoke so they could hear each other over the din of chit-chat and bursts of laughter echoing in the large room. Their conversation veered away from important matters like magic and hardship and friendship as they discussed more trivial things, such as the terrible food on offer.

'Honestly,' Libby said, eyeing up a trough of lasagna, 'I wouldn't give that to our dog.'

'You haven't got a dog.'

'I know. But if I did have one, I wouldn't insult it by putting *that* in its bowl. Is there even any cheese on top of it?'

The stone-faced woman serving behind the counter gave the girls a dry look and said, 'You could always try the cottage pie. Maybe that'll meet your exacting standards of culinary expertise.'

'That doesn't look too bad,' Libby said, holding out her plate. 'Edible, at least.'

'Glad we've got something that interests you,' the woman said with a clear edge of sarcasm as she plopped a dollop on the plate. 'Veg and gravy? That's assuming they look up to standard, of course?'

'They do,' Libby said, narrowing her eyes at the woman.

'I'll go with the same,' Ava said.

After her plate had been filled, the girls got their drinks and began chatting to each other again as they moved away. They were so busy talking about the woman that they didn't see the two girls approaching from the right. Libby turned just in time to see the surprised look on Ruth's face as they collided with each other. Libby's tray upended and everything on it went down the front of Ruth's uniform.

For a moment they just looked at each other. Libby's eyes were wide, her mouth a shocked O of surprise. Ruth, on the other hand, looked ready to commit murder. Her hands were clenched into claws, her eyes filled with malice.

A few giggles could be heard around the room, which Ruth silenced with glares.

'Oh wow!' Amy said from beside her. 'Don't even try and tell us that you didn't do that on purpose!'

'I'm sorry!' Libby said, apologizing animatedly to Ruth. 'I didn't see you. Honest, I didn't.'

'Yeah, right,' Amy said.

Ruth shoved Libby hard enough to nearly knock her over. She would have gone down had it not been for some kids behind her. They held out their hands, arresting her backward momentum.

'She didn't do it on purpose!' Ava snapped at Ruth.

'Look at the state of me!' Ruth said, looking down at herself. 'You couldn't have got more food and drink down me if you'd tried!'

'Oh I'm sure she tried,' Amy put in.

'No she didn't!' Ava responded through gritted teeth. 'Stop stirring up trouble, you ... twit!'

'*Oooh!* The burn!' Amy said, putting a finger on her arm and making a sound like sizzling bacon. 'Is that really the best you can do, Greenwood? Pathetic ... Just *pathetic!*'

Actually, no, I can do a lot better than that! Ava thought as she launched her tray in Amy's direction.

What happened next felt like it was playing out in slow

motion. Amy sidestepped out of the way. Just as she did, a gap opened in the crowd that'd formed behind her and the stone-faced dinner lady appeared, wanting to know what all the fuss was about. Her eyes widened as she saw the tray coming toward her. And then everything collided with her white pinafore-covered large chest, spraying food and drink everywhere.

The eruption of laughter was immediate. It echoed around the room. Even Ruth, who was covered in food and drink herself, couldn't resist a chuckle.

'Oh dear,' Amy said, raising her voice to be heard above the noise, 'I think you're going to be in a *lot* of trouble for this.' She winked at Ava, which made her even angrier.

'I know you weren't impressed with the food,' the dinner lady said, still as stone-faced as ever, 'but throwing it everywhere seems like a bit of an overreaction to the quality that's provided.'

Ava was about to say something in response, but then the voice of Mrs Fernsby boomed out across the room, wanting to know what was happening. The crowd parted and then there she was, standing with her hands on her hips. She surveyed the situation with an expression like someone chewing on the bitterest of lemons.

'Now why am I not surprised to see you pair at the heart of this ruckus,' she said to Ruth and Amy, eyeing them up and down. 'Why are covered in food and drink, Ruth?'

'Because *they* threw their trays over us!' she said, glaring at Ava and Libby.

'I didn't do it on purpose!' Libby protested. 'It was an accident!'

'Yeah, right,' Ruth said, rolling her eyes.

'And was it an accident when you threw yours at me?' Amy asked Ava.

'No!' she replied. 'But you goaded me into it! You just wanted me to do something so I'd get a detention.'

Mrs Fernsby turned her attention to the dinner lady, who explained how she'd come to be in the state that she was in.

'I wasn't the intended target,' she said blandly.

'I can only apologize and give you leave to clean yourself up,' Mrs Fernsby said. 'Feel free to go home if you have to and I'll arrange cover for you at the serving area.'

The dinner lady nodded and then disappeared through the crowd.

'With regards to you lot,' Mrs Fernsby said, taking in all four girls one after the other, 'this is the second incident in a short space of time where I've had to deal with you having an altercation with each other in this dinner hall. And the previous encounter involved beverages being thrown around as well, if I remember rightly.'

'That wasn't our fault and neither is this,' Ruth said.

'You're always at the heart of any trouble,' Mrs Fernsby said, 'and yet, for one reason or another, it's never your fault.'

'*We* didn't throw any food!' Amy protested.

Mrs Fernsby's top lip twitched as she fixed her with a particularly icy stare. 'First of all, you can take some of that base out of your voice. Secondly, I think a good dose of detentions is in order as a deterrent to any further maliciousness taking place between you four. And you can take those angry looks off your faces for starters. You're lucky I'm not suspending all of you, which is what the next step will be if you persist with this silly rivalry you've developed. It wouldn't be so bad if it was just you lot who got covered in food, but poor Mrs Baldry has ended up plastered in it as well.'

'Can I go home to get changed?' Ruth said.

'No, you cannot!' Mrs Fernsby said.

'But I'm a mess!' Ruth said, gesturing toward her front, which was covered in bits of cottage pie. 'You told Mrs Baldry she can go home, so why not me?'

'Because she isn't in trouble like you are,' Mrs Fernsby replied. 'I'll get you a top from the stores and you can think yourself lucky that you'll be getting that.'

'I can't believe this!' Ruth said, getting more and more miffed. 'We didn't even do anything wrong and we're getting detentions! Just ask someone – anyone! – what happened and they'll tell you that we're not to blame.' She pointed at a small, mousey girl. 'Go on, tell her! Tell her what happened!'

'I didn't actually see what happened,' the mousy girl replied sheepishly. 'I was eating my food. I heard raised voices. When I turned around, you had food all over you.' She shrugged. 'I didn't see how it got there.'

Ruth gave her a look which suggested she was not happy with her. Not happy at all. It was an "I'll deal with you later" look ...

Selecting another witness with a jab of her finger, Ruth demanded that an older, tall, skinny boy give an account of events. But all he could offer was a splaying of his hands and a simple: 'Nope – I didn't see either.'

'Well, someone must have seen!' Ruth raged as she looked at the crowd, prompting different students to speak up.

Of course they did, Ava thought. *But they don't want to help you because you're a bullying turd face.*

'Okay, I've had enough of my time being wasted here!' Mrs Fernsby said. She beckoned the crowd of students to disperse and get back to what they were doing with quick flicks of her fingers. 'And as for you four,' she said to the girls, 'any more trouble between you and I *will* be looking at suspension.' She got a nod from each of them as she looked at them in turn. 'I'll check my diary to see when's best for the detentions and let you know by the end of the day.'

Ruth skulked away with a look of thunder on her face. Amy trailed behind her.

Another dinner lady appeared and began cleaning up the mess on the floor.

'It should be you who's cleaning that up,' Mrs Fernsby said to Libby.

The headmistress gave both girls a disappointed look and then swept from the room, her shoe heels tapping out a rhythmic beat as she made her way past lots of lingering students.

'I'm sorry,' Libby said to Ava with a sheepish expression, 'that was all my fault. I should have looked where I was going. As if things weren't bad enough between us and those idiots ... And now I've made things even worse – probably *twice* as worse.'

'What's done is done,' Ava said, putting a reassuring hand on her shoulder. 'There's nothing we can do about it now.' Her lips cracked into a smile. 'Did you see the look on her face, though? Honestly, if I had a photo of that, I'd frame it and put it on my bedroom wall. It would brighten my day every time I looked at it.'

Libby smiled herself, but it disappeared as she said, 'My parents were miffed with me when I told them I had one detention, so how am I going to explain to them that I've got some more? My dad, *especially*, will not be happy when he finds out. There'll be questions, questions, questions. He'll want to know *everything*. And if I tell him that I'm being bullied he'll be straight into this school, having a go at Mrs Fernsby.'

'Would that be a bad thing? She might *do* something about Ruth and Amy then.'

'My dad is a bit like Willow's mum. He can be way over the top sometimes, so I'd just rather he didn't come anywhere near this place, to be honest. And I think Mrs Fernsby is doing about the best she can where those pair are concerned. She's given them some detentions when they didn't even do anything wrong, so that's a bonus. And she did say that the next step will be suspensions, so there's that to consider as well. No way will Ruth and Amy be able to avoid getting in trouble again, so it's only a matter of time before they both get kicked out of the school, I think.'

'Fingers crossed that it happens. The threat of suspensions was aimed at us as well, though. We need to make sure we don't get in any more trouble because I really wouldn't want to have to explain *that* to my parents.' Ava looked down at her tray of food. 'Do know what, I've lost my appetite. Are you going to get some more food or should we just bog off outside into the playground?'

'I've lost my appetite, too. And people are still staring at us, so, yeah, let's bog off.'

The girls left the room and spent most of the remainder of dinner time huddled in the far corner of the playground, talking about this and that. Ruth and Amy spotted them at one point, but they did not approach. Ruth had changed her sweater for a clean one, but the top of her skirt was still a smeared mess.

'She'll hate having to walk around looking like that,' Libby noted.

'I know,' Ava replied, grinning. 'It's great, isn't it?'

'For now, yes,' Libby said. 'But we both know that she'll already be plotting her revenge. And threats of detention, suspension or even being expelled won't stop her from trying to get that revenge. When Willow comes back, she'll be targeting her even more than before as well. All because of me. Damn! Why couldn't I have just been looking where I was going! And of all the people I could have bumped into, why did it have to be her?'

'What's done is done. As I said before, there's nothing we can do about it now.'

13.

Toward the end of the day, Mrs Fernsby caught up with the two girls as they were leaving their PE lesson. She pulled them to one side and gave them the bad news: three hour-long detentions in a row, beginning Thursday.

The girls' faces dropped. And the penny dropped as well …

'Three in a row?' Libby said. 'But that would mean that the last one is on Saturday?'

'That's right,' Mrs Fernsby confirmed with a smile playing at the corners of her lips.

'But the school isn't even open on weekends!' Ava blurted.

'It is if I'm here,' Mrs Fernsby said. 'I have lots of work to catch up on so it's no skin off my nose to be here. The first two detentions will be after school in room 34. The Saturday one will be a lot more … shall we say, labor intensive. It'll be a good chance for you to work and bond with Ruth and Amy.'

Libby's face dropped. 'Bond? With those pair? Are you kidding me?'

'Do I look like I'm joking?' Mrs Fernsby said sternly. 'Perhaps now you'll think twice before getting into any more trouble. I've informed your parents and they're okay with my plans. They're very concerned, as you can imagine, so you'll have some explaining to do when you get home, no doubt.' She turned swiftly on one heel and began to walk away. 'Oh, and don't be late,' she added. 'You know how much of a stickler I am for promptness!'

Ava waited until she was out of earshot, then said, 'She's informed our parents! Oh great! As soon as I get through the door, my mum will be all over me, wanting to know every detail. And then my dad will bombard me with questions when he gets in as well. That's all I need!'

'And I'm in for the same, too – but probably worse. Can my life get any worse!'

'Never tempt fate by saying something like that.'

14.

When Ava arrived home, she entered through the front door as quietly as possible and began tiptoeing toward the staircase. She was just about to put her foot on the first step when the living room door flung open and Mrs Greenwood appeared with her arms folded across her chest. She looked at Ava quizzically, asking a question without saying a word.

'It's not my fault,' Ava said, letting her bag drop to the floor.

'I think me and your father will be the ones to decide that,' Mrs Greenwood said. 'But I'm willing to give you the benefit of the doubt – for the moment, at least – because you're my daughter and you've never been in trouble before.' She gestured for Ava to speak. 'And don't tell any lies. All I ask is that you be truthful and I'll have your back against anybody.'

I'll have your back against anybody ... Those words sent shivers of pride through Ava, even though she'd planned to tell nothing but the truth.

She explained how there'd always been a problem with Ruth bullying her and Libby. 'But things have been worse over the last week or so,' Ava explained, 'ever since we made friends with the new girl at the school. Ruth and her sidekick, Amy, targeted Willow as soon as they laid eyes on her. And because we're pally with her, we're now attracting even more heat than we were before ...'

'And why are they targeting this Willow? Is it just because she's the new girl, or is that just part of it?'

'Her being new is part of it, I'd say. But I think the main reason is that Willow clearly comes from a poor family. You can just tell from her clothes, her bag, everything about her screams poor.'

Mrs Greenwood nodded to show that she understood the situation. 'Things never change, it seems,' she said. 'There's always a tier system at school: those at the top – the oppressors – and those at the bottom – the oppressed. To my knowledge, there's only ever been one way to deal with the bullies – the oppressors – and that's to stand up to them.'

'That's what we've been doing. And that's how we've ended up in detention.' Ava explained about the two dinner hall incidents and how Libby had accidentally collided with Ruth, spilling her tray of food down her. 'And, yes, before you ask, it was an accident. There's no way Libby would ever throw her food over anybody, never mind the school's apex predator.'

Mrs Greenwood unfolded her arms. Her expression softened as she took a moment to process everything she'd been told. 'It sounds as if me and your father need to pay a trip to the school to have a word with your headmistress,' she said. 'And don't look at me like that, young miss. I know it'd be embarrassing to have us rock up while you're there, so we'll do it after school when all the kids have gone home. Mrs Fernsby will still be there. The staff don't just hightail it out of there after you lot have gone, you know. They have stuff to sort out before they can go home.'

Ava relaxed a little. The idea of her parents rocking up at school had filled her with dread. But if they arrived after quarter to four then that would be fine. The school would be almost emptied of kids by that time.

'That'll be fine,' she said. 'Is it okay if I go to my room now?'

'Yes. Sure.'

Ava went to go up the stairs …

'Oh, one last thing,' Mrs Greenwood said. 'If you ever have any problems like this again, please tell us about it. If we know you've got problems then we can do something about them. I get why you haven't. Nobody wants their embarrassing parents involved in such things, but look how things have got out of control without some intervention. Can I get a promise?'

There's been intervention from Mrs Fernsby and look how that's worked out so far, Ava thought. But she nodded and gave her word anyway. Anything to keep her mum happy.

'Can I go now?' Ava said.

'Yes. Go on – skedaddle. I'll deal with your father when he gets in – make him understand.'

Ava skedaddled up to her room and crashed out on her bed.

She was still nervous about her father arriving home from work, despite her mother's assurances that she would make him understand. Sometimes he came back in a good mood and sometimes it was just wise to keep out of his way. Fortunately, he sounded chirpy as Ava listened to him moving about downstairs. Whistling was a good sign – and he was doing plenty of that.

It was about fifteen minutes later when he knocked on the bedroom door and entered.

'Your mother tells me you've been having problems at school with some other girls,' he said, 'and that you got yourself an undeserved detention.'

'Three undeserved detentions,' Ava said, correcting him.

'Three?' Mr Greenwood said, surprised. 'Your mother didn't say anything about *that*.' His expression hardened and then softened in an instant. 'But I guess that's by-the-by. The main thing to concentrate on is the fact that we've got your back where this is concerned. Your mother believes that you're not at fault and so do I. You've never been in trouble at school – *ever*. You're not that type. And neither is your friend Libby. Hopefully her parents will adopt the same approach as us and not stand for this. Your mother and I are going to give that headmistress of yours an earful. Make her see the error of her ways.'

Ava sat up and gave her dad a searching look. 'When you say "make her see the error of her ways",' she said, 'what exactly do you mean? You're not going to yell at her, are you? Because I don't think that'll work with Mrs Fernsby; she's a bit of a dragon and no soft touch, I can tell you.'

'We're just going to talk to her … in an assertive way,' Mr Greenwood said as he made his way across the room and planted a kiss on the top of his daughter's head. 'And don't worry,' he added as he was going back through the door, 'it'll all work out fine in the end. You'll see. Don't doubt your old dad – because you know he knows best.'

Ava wanted to express further concerns about taking a hardline approach with Mrs Fernsby, but her dad was gone before any words could leave her mouth. She briefly considered going after him, but she didn't bother. Once her father had made up his mind that he was going to do something, there was no going back. What would be would be – and that was that …

15.

In the morning, as Ava was getting ready to leave for school, her dad popped his head around the bedroom door and asked if she was okay.

'Yes,' she replied, trying to sound as chirpy as possible. 'Don't worry about me; I'll be fine.'

'If those girls try to start any trouble with you, just walk away, yeah? Go find a teacher. Don't worry about looking like a snitch. Just don't go getting in any more trouble when me and your mother will be talking to the headmistress later. Are we clear?'

'Crystal,' Ava said with a determined nod.

And a bit later, as she was about to go out of the front door, her mother said pretty much the same to her and then added: 'Your dad is leaving work early so he can attend this meeting. He's quite fired up and ready to take on your headmistress. You won't be doing three detentions, I can tell you. This is all assuming that you've been telling the truth with regards to everything that's happened, of course. You have told us everything, haven't you? You haven't missed out any details that she'll surprise us with? We don't want to be made to look like fools, Ava.'

'I haven't missed out any details. The worst she can say about me and Libby is that we reacted when we should have just walked away or got help from a teacher. And, no, Libby did not throw her tray of food over Ruth on purpose. Like I said before, she wouldn't do something like that; she just *wouldn't*. You've known her for years. Could you see her doing something like that?'

'No,' Mrs Greenwood said without hesitation, 'which is

why I haven't asked you if she did it on purpose.' She gave her daughter a smile and nod of confidence. 'Look, you just get yourself to school and keep out of trouble, yeah? I bet Libby's parents are just as livid as we are. I wouldn't be surprised if they pay Miss Fernsby a visit as well, don't you think?'

'Let's hope that they do,' Ava said, edging her way down the path as an indicator that she needed to get going.

Mrs Greenwood advanced to the doorway, raised her hand and smiled again. Her expression communicated a clear message that had already been spoken: we've got your back, Ava.

Returning the smile, Ava once again felt a surge of affection for her parents as she took off down the street at a brisk pace.

16.

Ava felt positive as she went through the school gates – and even more positive when she saw Libby talking to Willow in the playground. That positivity soon disappeared, however, when Ava noticed Ruth and Amy lurking by the bike sheds, looking on with suspicious smirks on their faces.

'Good to see you back,' Ava said to Willow as she was approaching her. 'And good to see that you're looking a lot better.'

Ava still didn't think that Willow looked one hundred percent. Her face was slightly drawn and there were dark marks beneath her eyes. The sort you get when you haven't been sleeping well. But Ava didn't think that her appearance had anything to do with a lack of sleep. *It's because you've been doing magic, isn't it?* she thought. *You just couldn't resist.* She decided not to say anything about this, though. Now was not the time.

'I definitely feel a lot better,' Willow said, smiling.

Libby filled her in on everything that'd happened while she'd been absent: the run-ins, the tray incident, the detentions.

'You've got *three* back-to-back detentions?' Willow said, gobsmacked. 'I don't know of anyone else who's ever had three. Oh, I wish I could have been there to see you chuck food over Ruth,' she said to Libby. 'That's just hilarious.'

'I didn't do it on purpose,' she replied, trying unsuccessfully to suppress a grin. 'I just turned around and she was there. It was an accident.'

'Of course it was,' Willow said, giving her a playful nudge and wink.

'No, really, it was an accident,' Libby was keen to stress.

'Three in a row,' Willow said, pondering the detentions. 'That's got to be some sort of record, yeah?'

'That's not a record we want to hold,' Ava said. 'My parents are not happy with Mrs Fernsby. They're coming to school after home time to have it out with her. I'll be interested to see how *that* plays out.'

'Mine aren't happy either,' Libby said. 'They're going to ring up today and give our headmistress an earful.'

'I wouldn't be surprised if you don't end up doing those detentions,' Willow said.

'You haven't been at this school long enough to know how much of a dragon Mrs Fernsby is,' Ava told her. 'I wouldn't be surprised if she doesn't back down. We'll find out soon enough.'

'Fingers crossed is all I can say,' Libby put in. She nodded toward Ruth and Amy. 'Three hour-long bonding sessions with those pair sounds like my idea of hell. It won't solve anything.'

'You're going to be in detention with those pair,' Willow said, glancing over at them. 'Good luck with that. Yikes! Which evenings?'

'Thursday and Friday,' Ava said. 'And Saturday morning,' she added with a roll of her eyes.

Willow's mouth dropped open. 'You're going to have to come to school on Saturday? Wow! That sucks. And neither of you have done anything wrong. I'd be really miffed if I were you guys.'

'That fact that we haven't done anything wrong is what sucks the most,' Libby said. 'And it's all because of those pair over there,' she added, nodding toward the school bullies again.

'Err, yeah, it's probably not a good idea to keep looking at them when they're glaring at us,' Ava said. 'Oh, great, they're coming over here now. Right, time to disappear.' She tried to get the other two to move but they wouldn't budge.

'What's the point of running away?' Libby said. 'We all

have lessons with them, so we may as well just deal with them now and get it over and done with.'

'Libby is right,' Willow said, holding her chin high as a mark of defiance. 'And if she can't get to us in lessons, there's always break time and dinner. They'll beef with us if they want to. We just need to make sure we don't beef back. Plus, it'll look cowardly if we skulk off. They'll think that we're scared of them.'

'We are scared of them,' Libby muttered.

'Speak for yourself,' Willow said, turning to face the advancing bullies.

Ava and Libby exchanged a look just as Ruth and Amy descended on them.

'Why do you keep looking at us?' Ruth said, glaring mostly at Ava. 'Is there something you want to say?'

'Why would we want to talk to you?' Willow said, doing some glaring of her own. She slid her bag off her back to hold it by the top handle.

You've brought the book with you, haven't you? Ava thought. *You've brought Shadowbound to school.*

'*Oooh!* The little mouse speaks,' Amy said to Willow. 'Have you grown a backbone while you've been off?'

Libby held up a hand as a calming gesture. 'How about we try and be friendly towards each other,' she suggested.

'We just want to know why you keep looking at us, is all,' Ruth said, showing a keen interest in Willow's bag. 'And why have you slid that bag off? Have you got something interesting in there? Something you can use as a weapon?'

'I bet it's a rounders bat or something,' Amy said, now showing a keen interest as well. 'That'll explain why you're so gobby and brave all of a sudden. Gonna bosh us, are you? Gonna smash us up, yeah?'

She can do a lot worse than that, Ava thought.

'There's nothing in my bag that would interest you,' Willow said, clutching it protectively to her stomach.

'*Oooooh!*' Amy said, pulling an annoying face. 'The little mouse has spoken again. She must have eaten all of her Weetabix this morning to be *this* brave!'

'Just leave her alone,' Ava said.

'And now the other mouse speaks,' Ruth said.

'Hmm, more like a rat,' Amy said, putting a finger on her chin in mock contemplation. She clicked her fingers together. 'Yep – definitely a rat.'

Ruth nodded in agreement. 'You never answered my question,' she said, edging closer to Ava. 'Why were you looking at us, eh? Why were you gawking at us ... you little rat!'

'Leave her alone!' Willow said, stepping in front of her to form a barrier.

A tall figure appeared to the right and everyone turned to see Mrs Fernsby looming over the situation. 'Well, well, well, it's you lot again,' she said, looking from one girl to another. 'Apparently three detentions aren't enough of a deterrent to keep you away from each other. Is there an ounce of common sense between the lot of you? What part of staying away from each other did you not get?'

'They were staring at us,' Amy said, levelling an accusatory finger mostly at Ava.

'We weren't staring,' Willow said. 'We did look at you, yes – but that's only because we're worried about you. We don't want you sneaking up on us or anything. Funnily enough, we don't trust you.'

'And we don't trust you either!' Ruth blurted.

'*Quiet!*' Mrs Fernsby snapped.

This got some attention. Other students stopped what they were doing to gawk.

Mrs Fernsby closed her eyes for a second. She inhaled, held her breath for a moment, then exhaled – calming herself. 'I'm going to give you lot one last chance,' she said. 'Stay away from one another. Don't talk to one another – don't even look at one another. One more incident such as this and I'll be down on you like a skip full of rubble! Am I making myself clear here?'

Libby was first to answer: 'Yes, miss!'

Then the others followed suit.

'I don't hold out much hope for you,' Mrs Fernsby said, 'so let's see if you can prove me wrong.' She checked her watch. 'The bell is about to sound, so you may as well begin making your way inside.'

Ruth and Amy stormed away, looking severely miffed.

Ava, Libby and Willow made their way toward the main entrance under the watchful eye of Mrs Fernsby.

The bell sounded as they entered the foyer.

'They seem determined to get us all expelled,' Ava said.

'They're going to drag us down with them,' Libby added.

Other students began piling through the door, so the girls moved to the other side of the foyer so they were out of the way.

'We just need to do what Mrs Fernsby has told us to do,' Ava said, continuing the conversation. 'Steer well clear and ignore them as much as we can (although we didn't do a very good job of ignoring them just now).'

'It won't be that easy,' Willow said. 'There's a score to settle where that tray of food incident is concerned. Ruth and her sidekick won't let that slide. They'll be plotting something. I haven't been at this school for long and I don't know either of them well, but I know enough to say with some degree of certainty that ignoring them won't change anything.'

'So what do you suggest?' Libby asked her.

'Why are you lot lingering here?'

The girls turned to see Mr Shaw watching them from by the door. 'You'll be late for your lessons,' he added, clapping his hands together. 'Get a move on! Chop, chop!'

They scurried down the hallway so they could distance themselves from him. They stopped at the south stairwell and Libby stood on the bottom step as they continued to discuss things for a few more minutes

'Look, we'll talk more about everything at break time,' Ava said as she and Willow kept moving along the corridor. 'The only thing we need to concentrate on between now and then is not beefing with the idiots, yeah?'

'No beefing,' Libby said. She gave a nod as her answer and then took off up the stairs in a blur of movement.

'I'm pretty sure we're going to be late,' Willow said as she and Ava pushed through some double doors.

'I'm pretty sure you're right. Good job we've only got Mr Jones to worry about and not one of the stricter teachers.'

'Even so, I don't like going into class late. Everybody stares at you. I *hate* being the center of attention.'

'You and me both.'

By the time they reached the classroom, the door was closed and the lesson was underway.

Willow slipped her bag off her back and held it by the top handle.

Ava couldn't help but notice how she was keeping it protectively close to herself.

'Just put your head down and go straight to your seat,' Ava advised as she looked through the glass in the top half.

Ruth and Amy were sitting in their usual places: together at the back of the classroom. *Oh, they're going to love this*, Ava thought.

She didn't waste another second, though. Pushing the door open, she moved briskly across the room. She heard the door click shut and looked up to see Willow walking to her desk.

The teacher was at the front of the room, by the whiteboard. Ava was dismayed to see that it was Miss Becker. She wondered why it was her and not Mr Jones.

'Get lost, did you?' Miss Becker said, directing her

question mostly at Willow because she was closest. 'Or did you oversleep? Or were you so busy talking to each other that you lost track of the time? Those are the three usual excuses.'

As Willow turned her head to reply, she stubbed her toe on a desk leg and went sprawling. Her bag escaped her grasp and slid across the floor. The reaction from all the kids was immediate: an eruption of laughter which echoed around the room. It lasted a few seconds, but to Willow, it must have felt like much longer.

And then Miss Becker told everyone to shut up: '*Be QUIET! SHUT YOUR MOUTHS! NOW! AND WHEN I SAY NOW, I MEAN NOWWWW!*'

Silence descended as Willow got back to her feet. For a few seconds she just stood there, rooted to the spot, looking around at everyone with a vacant expression on her face. Ava could see tears beginning to well in her eyes. She was about to go to her, but then Willow got moving and retrieved her bag. As she picked it up, however, something fell out and plopped to the floor. Ava couldn't see what it was, but she figured that it could only be the Shadowbound, judging by the mortified look on Willow's face as she bent down to retrieve the item. And then Ava did catch a glimpse of it as Willow stowed it hastily back in her bag.

'Are you okay?' Miss Becker asked her, showing a level of concern that Ava had never seen before.

'I'm fine,' Willow replied, looking anything but so as she brushed herself off.

A low snicker of laughter from the back of the classroom caught her attention. Her fingers teased toward the zip on her bag as she glared at Ruth with increasing intensity.

Trying to catch her attention, Ava shook her head at her, silently mouthing the words: 'No, don't do it – she's not worth it. *Don't do it!*'

Then Miss Becker put a hand on Willow's shoulder and told her to sit down. Ava relaxed and let out a gasp of relief as she watched Willow do as she was instructed.

'Really?' Miss Becker said, addressing the class as a whole, 'is that what we do when someone hurts themselves? *Laugh* at them? You should be ashamed, the lot of you. How would you feel if that happened to you?' She looked past Ava. 'And you, Ruth Ribble, would do well to keep a low profile. I'm well aware of your situation and how much trouble you're in. *All* the staff are aware – just so you know.'

'But I haven't said or done anything!' she protested.

'Of course you haven't,' Miss Becker said with a sarcastic smile. With a hint of compassion in her expression, her eyes lingered on Willow for a second and then the lesson continued as though nothing had happened. Ava learned that Miss Becker was covering for Mr Jones, who was absent due to illness.

At the end, as everyone was filing out, Miss Becker asked Willow to stay behind so she could have a word with her. Ava stood next to Willow, hoping that she could be part of the conversation that was about to take place.

'There's no reason for you to be here,' Miss Becker said,

gesturing for Ava to leave.

'But I know about everything that's happened where Ruth is concerned,' she said.

'I'm sure you do,' Miss Becker said, 'but I don't need your input. So, please ...' she shooed Ava away, 'be on your way. And close the door behind you.'

Ava did as she was instructed and then waited in the corridor, by the door, so she could earwig. She shuffled to the side, her shoes squeaking slightly on the floor.

A few seconds later, Miss Becker stuck her head out and asked her why she was lingering.

'I ... erm ...'

'Just get yourself off into the playground or something,' she snapped, 'before I lose my patience.'

As Ava walked away, she heard the door slam shut behind her. The sound of it echoed into the corridor, making her jump. She kept walking but then stopped. She desperately wanted to know what they were talking about, but she didn't want to incur any further wrath from Miss Becker. *Just keep walking*, Ava thought, *and Willow will tell you about it later*.

Realizing that she was going the wrong way, she turned around and headed back.
She moved as quickly and soundlessly as possible past the classroom where Miss Becker was talking to Willow about ... something (bullying, most likely – and how to deal with it).

Curiosity was still gnawing at Ava, so she brought herself to a halt. She checked left and right and was pleased to see that no one else was around. *I just need to be quiet*, Ava thought as she edged toward the door and positioned herself by the wall to the right, out of sight. *Super quiet.*

'I just want to see the book that's in your bag,' Miss Becker was saying to Willow. 'There's no reason to be defensive. I just want to establish whether what you've got there is what I think it is.'

'It's just a book about magic,' Willow responded.

'I know it is; I heard you the first time. And I'll repeat what I said before. I'm not going to take it from you. I just want a look – a *peek*. You can extend me that much of a courtesy … yes? I'm just trying to help.'

Ava couldn't resist looking through the glass. She saw Willow hesitantly opening her bag and pulling out the book to show Miss Becker, who was eyeing it with what could only be described as an ominous expression.

'A collection of dark spells,' she said to Willow. 'Where did you get this?'

'The Book Cove in town,' she replied nervously. 'Have you been in there?'

'Alas, no, I come from Derby. I'm one of the poor unfortunates who has to commute some distance to work and back every day, so I don't know the local area well at all. Now, with regards to the book, you found it in the magical section, I take it?'

Willow nodded.

'Did you feel compelled to buy it? Drawn to it, somehow? As if you must have it, no matter what?'

Looking increasingly sheepish, Willow nodded again.

'Ah ... okay,' Miss Becker said, sporting a concerned expression. 'So the next obvious question is: have you attempted any of the spells? Judging by the look of you, I'm guessing the answer is yes.'

Willow confirmed this with another nod.

'O-kay,' Miss Becker said again, taking a moment to process this information. Then she leaned forward and locked eyes with Willow. 'You need to get rid of that book. It's evil. It'll suck the life out of you. But then I think you already know that. It's latched on to you but it's not really for you. It's meant to be owned by a dark wizard or witch, who'll be able to use it without the problems you're experiencing. And when this book does finally fall into the hands of that wizard or witch, they'll draw on the power it collected from you. Do you want that to happen?'

'No, of course not,' Willow said, horrified by the idea.

'Then give it to me,' Miss Becker said, holding out her hand.

Willow backed away a step, then another. 'No ... I can't,' she said. 'This book is the most amazing thing that's ever happened to me – that will probably *ever* happen to me – so I'm not handing it over to anybody.'

'Even with what I've told you,' Miss Becker said, 'you still want to keep it, knowing what it'll do to you?'

Willowed looked lost, confused, bewildered. 'I ... I don't know what to do,' she said. 'But who's to say that you're not a dark witch.' Willow took another step back. 'Why should I trust you? Why should I trust anybody who wants to take this book away from me?'

'I can understand you being cautious,' Miss Becker said, 'but ...' she reached into her bag at the side of her desk, pulled out another book and showed it to Willow, 'I can trade you almost like for like. The only difference is that this one won't drain the life out of you. It's a normal book of spells.' She held it out for Willow to take. 'For any darkness in this world, there is always an equal and opposite capable of banishing it. What I'm offering you is that opposite. Anything that can be done with that book you're holding can be done with this one.'

'You're a witch?' Willow said, awestruck.

And she wasn't the only one who was feeling awestruck, either. Ava was looking on with the same gob-smacked expression as her friend. *She's a witch!* she thought. *No way – no frickin' way! Miss Becker is* actually *a witch as well!*

The teacher answered Willow's question with a spell. She made the book that she was holding float over to Willow and hang in mid-air in front of her.

'Spells for the Inquisitive Mind by Loren Serenson,' Willow said, reading the title and author name.

'All you need to do is a simple exchange,' Miss Becker said, offering a rare smile, 'and you'll feel so much better for it.'

Willow's eyes were wide as she looked at the floating book, weighing up her options. She reached out to take it but then paused. 'But you really could be a dark witch,' she said, 'and this could just be a trick to get my book away from me.'

'Oh my dear child,' Miss Becker said, 'I've been doing magic for nearly forty years. If I wanted to take that book from you, I'd take it. And there isn't a thing you could do to stop me. What I want is for you to willingly give it to me, because that will help break the bond you're forging with that evil book. The longer it remains in your possession, the harder it will be to break that bond. You're lucky that you've only had it for a short while. But even so, look at what it's done to you in that period of time. Do the right thing, Willow. It's a simple exchange.'

Ava didn't know what to make of this. What if Miss Becker was indeed a dark witch? What then? *What if she can't take the book from Willow? What if it has to be given willingly from one witch to another for ownership to be exchanged? And what if the book that's floating in front of Willow isn't a real magic book? What if it's just a decoy? An ordinary book disguised as a magical one?* These and a lot more questions were swirling around inside Ava's head as she looked on, resisting an increasing urge to burst into the room.

'You haven't known me for long, so I get the lack of trust,' Miss Becker said to Willow. 'And your impression of me so far is probably that I'm quite a cold person, hardline, authoritarian: which might make you think that I'm not a good person. But I am the way I am because I believe in discipline and respect. Without the former, there can be no latter. The kids I teach would walk all over me if I gave them an inch, so I don't even give them that. But as hardline as I am, I will always be there for any student who needs my help. That's why I got into teaching: because I wanted to make a difference by helping youngsters be the best that they can be. You just need to let me help you by taking that book away from you and giving you one that suits your soul – your *good* soul.'

Miss Becker moved the levitating book slightly closer to Willow.

And that's when Ava heard a noise coming from down the corridor. She looked to her right and saw Mr Parkes coming toward her.

'Shouldn't you be outside by now?' he said as he reared up in front of her, towering over her with his lanky frame.

'I … err,' Ava said, attempting to think up a plausible explanation for her loitering and coming up with nothing.

'Something interesting happening in there, is there?' he said, stooping forward to peer into the classroom.

'My friend's in there,' Ava replied, 'and I'm just waiting for her to come out.'

'Ah, right,' Mr Parkes said, scratching absently at the side of his nose. 'And does your friend know that you're waiting? What about Miss Becker? Is she aware of your presence?'

'Erm … no and no,' Ava said. She got an overwhelming feeling that this awkward situation was about to become even more awkward.

And then it did. Mr Parkes opened the door and asked Miss Becker if she was aware that an onlooker was lingering in the corridor, even though he knew full well the answer to that question.

'No, I wasn't aware,' Miss Becker said, regarding Ava with raised eyebrows and an otherwise unreadable expression.

Busted!

Willow, on the other hand, was sporting a very readable expression: one of concern.

Is that because you've handed over the Shadowbound and don't know whether you've done the right thing? Ava thought. *Or is it because you didn't hand it over and aren't sure whether you did the right thing?*

There was no sign of either of the books. They'd disappeared from view as if they'd been magicked away (which could well have been the case, Ava thought).

'Don't worry,' Miss Becker said to Mr Parkes, 'I'll deal with this. I'm already sorting out one troubled child, so why not add another, eh?'

Mr Parkes gave her a nod and shut the door as he left.

Miss Becker waited a moment, then got up and went to the door herself. She peered left and right through the glass. Satisfied with what she saw, she went back to her desk and fell quite heavily into her seat.

'So,' she said, looking from one girl to the other, 'who wants to talk first?'

Ava saw no point in lying, so she said, 'I was lingering outside because I wanted to see whether Willow exchanged the evil book of spells for the one that you were making float in mid-air.'

Willow opened her bag and pulled out the one that'd

been floating. 'It was a fair exchange,' she said, 'and one that should be good for my health.'

'It will *definitely* be better for your health,' Miss Becker said. ' Her expression hardened as she looked from one girl to the other. 'So who else knows about all this? How many memories am I going to have to wipe?'

Ava could feel the blood draining out of her face. 'What?' she said, aghast at the idea of having her memory wiped. 'There's no need for that! Why would you do that?'

'Because,' Miss Becker said, 'we magical folk are a tight-knit community. The fewer people who know about what we can do, the better. We don't need blabbermouths telling everyone. The last thing we need is attention – for obvious reasons.' She looked at Willow. 'That's the first thing you should learn where magic is concerned.'

'I haven't told lots of people,' she said. 'Just Ava and Libby.'

'Libby Hargreaves?' Miss Becker said.

'Yes,' Willow replied.

'Well, at least that's some good news,' Miss Becker said. 'It'll make things nice and easy for me with it only being two (that's assuming you're telling the truth, of course).'

'Nice and easy?' Ava said. 'What, for when you wipe mine and Libby's memories, you mean?' She instinctively took a few steps back, then realized there was no point in fleeing. *She's a witch*, she thought. *If she wants to wipe my memory, she'll do it – and there won't be a thing I can do to stop her*.

'Oh it'll be quite painless,' Miss Becker informed her, 'so

you have nothing to worry about. You won't know anything about it; I'll just catch you when you're not expecting it and that'll be that, as they say.'

'I don't want my memory wiped,' Ava said sternly. 'And neither will Libby.'

Miss Becker offered an apologetic smile and said, 'I'm sorry, but what's got to be done has got to be done. I have to take into consideration both your and Libby's recent behavior as well. I've overheard things being said about both of you in the staffroom. Not good things. It would appear that you pair have been going off the rails for one reason or another recently, which is not good.'

'They've been getting into trouble because they've been defending themselves against the school bully,' Willow said, moving in front of her friend. 'And it'll be pointless ... because I'll tell them both what happened to them. So they'll know everything anyway, no matter what you do. If they don't believe me, I can always do some spells to convince them.'

The smile disappeared from Miss Becker's face and was replaced by a scowl. 'That would be a very foolish thing to do,' she said, almost hissing the words out. *Very* foolish indeed. Perhaps I should go one step further and wipe *your* memory as well,' she said to Willow, 'because *that* will solve the problem – won't it?'

'I'm beginning to think that handing over that book of evil spells to you was a bad idea,' Ava said. She leaned in close to Willow and whispered in her ear: 'Please tell me you didn't give it to her?'

'I can hear you, you know,' Miss Becker said. 'I might be getting on a bit, but I'm not deaf. And, yes, she did give it to me.' She pulled the book out of her bag and then stowed it back away. 'You should have no fears about me being in possession of it. If I were a dark witch, you pair would already know about it by now. You'd have been dealt with, as the saying goes.' She held her hands up in a calming gesture. 'Look, with regards to the memory wipes, I'll think about it this evening and get back to you with a decision tomorrow. Maybe you can be trusted ... I just ... need to think. And don't worry, I won't hit you in the back with a spell when you're not looking, so you can relax for the rest of the day. You have my word.'

'But what will you do with that book?' Ava said, nodding toward the bag. 'You can't destroy it.'

'How do you know that?' Miss Becker asked, raising a quizzical eyebrow.

Ava explained how she and Libby had tracked down the previous owner so they could ask her for help. 'She looked terrible,' Ava said somberly. 'Like she'd aged by twenty or thirty years. And she wasn't much help. The best advice she offered was to take the book back to the shop and hope that some other witch or wizard would buy it so that the bond could be broken.'

'This witch,' Miss Becker said, 'where does she live and what's her name?'

Ava told her.

'Hmm,' Miss Becker said, pursing her lips together as she processed this information, 'I don't think I know her, but I can't entirely blame her for not wanting anything more to do with the book. She must have been very relieved when the bond was broken,' she looked at Willow, 'thanks to you.'

Willow took an interest in her feet. 'I didn't know what I was getting myself into when I bought that book. All I knew was that I had to have it. I didn't think for one second that I'd be able to do real magic.' She opened her bag and brightened as she pulled out the other book then showed it to Ava. 'But now I'll be able to do magic and not worry about having the life sucked out of me, so that's cool.'

'Cool, indeed,' Miss Becker said. 'And do you know what would be even cooler? If you had a book of potions and a wand as well. I'll bring them to school tomorrow.'

Willow grinned expectantly. 'A book of potions *and* a wand?' she said, jumping up and down, hardly able to contain her excitement. 'Wow – just *wow*!'

'Why does she need a wand?' Ava asked Miss Becker. 'She hasn't needed one so far.'

'You don't need one for the easy to medium spells,' she explained, 'but some of the more difficult ones will be a stretch to do without a wand. It helps to channel and intensify a witch or wizard's powers, so I would advise using one – especially if you're a beginner.'

'I will *definitely* use it!' Willow said.

'What about a broomstick?' Ava asked Miss Becker. 'You haven't got one of those knocking around, have you?'

'I don't have a spare one, I'm afraid,' she replied. 'But I do have a few wands, hence it not being too much trouble for me to part with one of them. You can't just ride any old broomstick, as you can imagine. Well, you could try - but you won't get very far. The nearest place to get magical supplies is The Mystic Magic in Wiggleswick. It's about five miles from here but well worth the trip. They've got everything you'll need: potion ingredients, charms, pendants, wands, broomsticks and lots of other stuff that'll blow your minds.' She looked at the clock on the wall and gasped at the time. 'Oh my, have we really been talking for that long? You should both scram along now while there's still something of your break left for you to enjoy.' Miss Becker motioned for the girls to show some hustle, so they did.

But then she added: 'You gave the book willingly to me, Willow, so I now have ownership. It will no longer call to you and you'll feel a lot better in yourself soon enough.'

'Thank you for freeing me from its grasp,' she replied. 'And thank you for the new book.'

'What will you do with the Shadowbound?' Ava asked Miss Becker.

'I don't know yet,' she replied. 'I know of the dangers involved and the temptations I'll face, but I could not leave this thing in your possession, knowing what it will do to you. I will need to be strong until I can figure out what to do with the accursed thing. And I'll have to do some research. Troubling and challenging times are ahead of me, I'm sure. But what must be done must be done, as the old saying goes.'

The girls went to leave but Ava lingered in the doorway and said, 'About the memory-wiping thing ...'

'I told you that I'd get back to you with a decision by tomorrow,' Miss Becker said, 'and that is what I will do. Please don't try and rush me. I need time to mull everything over, so scram along and let me do just that.'

Ava and Willow scrammed along. Willow couldn't contain her excitement as they were making their way hurriedly down the corridor.

'I can't believe what I'm going to get my hands on tomorrow,' she said, grinning, '*and* there's a magic shop not too far from here where I'll be able to get all sorts of things (assuming I can muster some money from somewhere). Will you come with me to the shop when I go? You and Libby, yeah? I'm sure there'll be stuff that you can buy, even though you're not magical.'

'Of course we'll come,' Ava said as they both pushed through a set of double doors.

'You don't look very excited?'

'Ah, well, the prospect of having my memory wiped has dampened my enthusiasm somewhat.'

Willow stopped as they reached the side exit. 'She won't do that to you and Libby, I'm sure. After she's thought about it, she'll realize that you can be trusted. I haven't known you pair that long and even I know *that*.'

17.

Ava and Willow met up with Libby in the far corner of the playground. It was a breezy, cloudy day. Occasionally the sun would break through, however, causing all three of them to squint.

'How come you pair are so late getting out here?' Libby said. 'I've been waiting here for nearly ten minutes!'

Ava and Willow looked at each other.

'Shall I tell her?' Ava said, beaming. 'Or do you want to do the honors?'

'You can tell her,' Willow said. 'I don't mind.'

'Don't mind what?' Libby said. 'What is it you need to tell me?'

'Well ...' Ava said, pausing dramatically for effect ...

Libby coaxed her on. 'Well what? Come on, just blurt it out! We haven't got long left, you know.'

'... Willow isn't the only witch at this school,' Ava finished.

Libby's mouth dropped open. 'Seriously? Who else is one then?' She looked at the kids on the playground.

'Nope,' Willow said, 'it's not a student.'

'One of the teachers?' Libby said.

'Yup,' Ava said, without elaborating.

'Oh, so I'm going to have to guess, right?' Libby didn't wait for an answer. 'Mrs Fernsby? It's gotta be her ...'

'Nope,' Ava said.

'Mr Shaw?'

'Nope,' Willow said.

'So who is it then?' Libby said. 'Come on, just tell me. The suspense is killing me!'

'Miss Becker,' Ava said.

'That old trout?' Libby said, gob-smacked. 'But how do you know? What's happened? How did you find out?'

Willow explained about how the Shadowbound had dropped out of her bag in class and how Miss Becker had caught a glimpse of it. 'And a glimpse was all she needed to know exactly what type of book it is,' she explained. 'So she asked me to stay behind after the lesson had finished and that's when she began quizzing me about it. She asked me where I'd got it from and if I'd attempted any of the spells. One thing led to another and then she produced another book of spells. One that isn't evil.' Willow opened her bag just enough so Libby could glimpse it. 'And so we did an exchange. I swapped the evil book for one that isn't going to destroy my health and suck the life out of me.'

'And what's Miss Becker going to do with the Shadowbound?' Libby said. 'Does she know how dangerous it is? That it'll make her ill if she does any of the spells?'

'She knew exactly what it was as soon as she laid eyes on it,' Willow said. 'And she's going to do some research to see what she can do with it.'

'So how come you were involved in the conversation between Willow and Miss Becker?' Libby asked Ava. 'How did *that* come about?'

Ava explained about how she'd been caught earwigging at

the classroom door by Miss Becker. 'She sent me away. But I was desperate to know what was being said, so I went back to the classroom to do some more earwigging. And that's what I was doing when Mr Parkes caught me and frog-marched me in to face Miss Becker. She told him that she'd deal with me and he bogged off. Miss Becker knew that I'd overheard and seen everything, so she had it out with me. The exchange of books had already taken place by then.'

'And this isn't the only book I'll be getting,' Willow said, giving Libby another flash of it in her bag. 'Miss Becker is going to give me one about potions. And – get this! Mega-mega exciting! – she's going to give me a wand, too.'

'No frickin way!' Libby said in awe. Her expression changed to one of confusion. 'But why would you need one? You haven't needed one to do magic so far?'

Ava explained how casting spells is easier with a wand. 'It will help focus and channel Willow's powers.'

'Cool,' Libby said.

'And apparently, there's a magic shop not far from here called The Mystic Magic where I'll be able to get all sorts of supplies,' Willow said.

'It's in Wiggleswick,' Ava added.

'I know where that is,' Libby said. 'I've been past it a few times on the bus to Bedlington. I've never given it much attention, though, to be honest (even though there's an awesome mural on the outside, depicting a dragon swooping down on a castle). Just when I think things can't get better, you keep telling me stuff that's more and more cool.'

'We need to tell her about the not-so-cool bit,' Willow said to Ava.

'What's this not-so-cool bit?' Libby said, concerned.

'Miss Becker is considering wiping our memories,' Ava told her.

'What?' Libby said, aghast. 'Why would she want to do that?'

'She's worried that we'll blab to people,' Ava said.

'And what have we done to make her think that we'll blab?' Libby blurted.

'She's heard bad things about us in the staffroom, apparently,' Ava said. 'Plus, she just doesn't think it's a good idea for non-magical people to know that witches and wizards exist.'

All the color had drained out of Libby's face. She looked worried, *deeply* worried. 'I *don't* want anyone messing with my memory,' she said angrily. 'She could mess the spell up and then I might not even know who I am!'

'Keep your voice down!' Ava said. 'Someone will hear you!'

'I told Miss Becker that it would be pointless wiping your memories,' Willow said, 'because I'd just fill you in about everything after she'd done the spell.'

'Ooooh – nice one!' Libby said, brightening. 'And what did she say to *that*?'

'She threatened to wipe my memory as well,' Willow said.

'Ah,' Libby said, looking troubled again as she began chewing on her bottom lip.

'She told us that she'll let us know one way or another by tomorrow,' Willow informed her.

'Oh great!' Libby said. 'So that'll be no sleep for me tonight then because I'll be too worried.' Something occurred to her. 'Hey, hang on a minute. Who's to say that Miss Becker isn't an evil witch? Who's to say that she hasn't just tricked her way into getting hold of that book by exchanging it for a fake?'

'That's what I thought at first,' Ava said. 'But it doesn't make sense when you think about it. Miss B wouldn't be carrying a fake magic book around with her on the chance that she might bump into someone with an evil one that she can exchange it for, would she? That sounds like a stretch to me.'

'It does, yeah,' Libby admitted. 'Unless she just had a normal one because she's never been able to get her hands on an evil one. I mean, how many evil ones are out there? We have no idea. They could be rare, for all we know.'

'That's true,' Willow said. 'But has Miss Becker ever done anything to suggest that she's evil?'

'Well, yeah,' Libby said, 'she's evil every day – miserable as hell and strict as hell too. If she smiled, her face would disintegrate, I'm sure.'

'Just because she's miserable and strict doesn't mean that she's evil,' Ava said.

'And she is giving me a wand and a potions book tomorrow,' Willow pointed out. 'That's not something an evil witch would do, is it?'

'Let's wait and see if you get them,' Libby said. 'Hey, I wonder if there are any other witches and wizards at this school? I bet Miss Becker isn't the only teacher who's magical. And I bet there are kids here that are magical.'

'You're probably right,' Willow said.

'I'd say there's reasonable odds that you and her aren't the only people who can do magic here,' Ava said. 'And it makes me wonder how many people at this school could have powers and not even know they've got them.'

'And not just at this school,' Libby said. 'I bet there are lots of people here, there and everywhere who have no idea of what they're capable of doing.'

'If only they knew,' Willow said. 'It would turn their lives upside down.'

Ava checked her watch. 'Okay, look,' she said, 'forget about all that for now. There's just one thing we need to concentrate on for the next day or so – and that's keeping an eye on Miss Becker.'

'What good is keeping an eye on her going to do?' Libby said. 'All she has to do is say a few magical words while looking at me and that'll be it – bam! – she'll have wiped my memory.'

'It's not that easy for her,' Ava said. 'She can easily decide what she wants to do about us. It's Willow that's the problem. Miss Becker won't know what to do where she's concerned.' Ava focused her attention on Willow. 'I doubt she'll want to wipe your memory as well. You're a witch, like her, so she'll feel some sense of loyalty to you. She knows that you'll tell us what's happened if she wipes our memories, so that's what she's puzzling over.'

'Loyalty or not,' Ava said, 'the safest thing for her to do would be to wipe *all* our memories of everything to do with any magical goings on. It's the easiest and most foolproof thing for her to do. Unless ...'

Libby and Willow looked at her, beckoning her to continue.

'... we solve the problem for her,' Ava finished saying.

'Solve the problem for her?' Libby said. 'But ... how?'

'Yeah, how?' Willow said. And then she realized. '*Oh, you want me to ...?*'

'Yep,' Ava said, nodding. 'It's something we've got to consider.'

Libby had caught on too. 'It seems a bit extreme.'

'What, and wiping *our* memories isn't extreme?' Ava said. 'The way I see it we have two options. One, we take our chances and hope she doesn't pull a sneaky on us. And two, we be the ones who do the sneaky with a pre-emptive strike.'

'A pre-what?' Libby said, frowning with confusion.

'She means that we wipe her memory first,' Willow clarified.

'Is that something you could do?' Ava asked her.

'Yeah, probably,' Willow replied. 'Assuming that it isn't an advanced spell and that it's actually in the book.' She fished it out of her bag and ran her finger down the index. 'Ah-hah! Yes. It's here.' She thumbed her way to the correct page.

'And ... it's a medium level one, so it shouldn't be a problem.'

'That's assuming that the book you have there isn't a fake dud, of course,' Libby pointed out.

'We need to know whether it is or not,' Ava said. 'And we need to know as soon as possible.'

The bell rang to signify the end of break time.

'Damn!' Ava said. 'We've still got so much to discuss. At dinner time, let's all rush to the hall so we can be first in the queue. We'll throw our food down our necks, then find somewhere quiet where you,' she nodded at Willow, 'can do a test spell, so we'll know one way or the other, yeah?'

'Okay,' Willow said, sliding her book safely back into her bag as they made their way across the playground.

'Sounds like a plan,' Libby said.

Willow said, 'I'll get there as fast as I can.'

'I'll be like a blur, I'll be so quick,' Libby said.

As they neared the building, Ava asked Willow which lesson she had next.

'Art. Literally the only subject that interests me.'

Ava opened her mouth to speak, but someone shoulder-barged past her, causing her to jolt forward.

'Ooops! Sorry!' Ruth said as she was passing with Amy. 'Didn't see you there.'

They both giggled as they disappeared through the entrance.

'Of course you didn't,' Ava said, seething.

'I can sort them out,' Willow said with a steely look in her eyes. 'All you have to do is say the word.'

'I am *so* tempted to say the word,' Libby said angrily.

'We'll discuss it at dinner time,' Ava said. 'Let's just take one thing at a time and get the next two lessons out of the way. The most important thing is that we keep trying to ignore Ruth and Amy, treat them like they don't exist.'

'You've got a lesson with them this afternoon,' Libby said, 'so that's going to be difficult.'

'I don't think I have,' Willow said. 'I need to check my timetable.' She went to reach into her bag ...

'Look, let's just get to our lessons,' Ava said. 'We don't want to be late and get any more black marks against our names.'

18.

At dinner time, Ava was the first to arrive in the hall. She lingered in the doorway, waiting for the other two. *Come on, where are you?* She thought. *You promised me you'd be quick!* And then they appeared in view, jogging toward her with smiles on their faces. Willow's bag was bobbing up and down on her back.

'What took you so long?' Ava said as they neared her.

'I came as quick as I could,' Willow said, slightly out of breath.

'Me too,' Libby said, puffing and panting. 'You obviously didn't have as far to go as us.'

'Whatever!' Ava said, gesturing along the corridor toward all the other students who were now coming their way. 'Let's just get our food and make it disappear.'

A few minutes later they were sitting at a table in the corner, scoffing pizza like it was a speed eating contest. Willow and Ava had chosen cheesecake for afters, whereas Libby had opted for ice cream and was struggling to eat it quickly.

'I told you to go for the cheesecake,' Ava said.

'I don't like it,' she replied. 'The words "cheese" and "cake" don't belong in the same sentence.'

'Have you ever tried some?' Willow asked her.

'Yes,' she responded, 'and I didn't like it.' She spooned a big gulp of ice cream into her mouth and swallowed it. Then she grimaced and began tapping the side of her head with her fingers. 'Oooooh! *Oooooh!* What an idiot!'

'What's up?' Willow said, concerned. 'Are you all right?'

'Brain-freeze,' Ava said, giggling.

'Brain … what?' Willow said.

'It's what you get when you eat something too quickly that's frozen,' Ava explained. 'You haven't had it before then, I take it?'

'No,' Willow said. 'But then I do like to take my time and savor my deserts, so …'

'Okay – heads up! It's time to leave,' Ava said, nodding toward Ruth and Amy, who'd just sauntered through the doorway. 'Let's get out of here before they notice us.'

Ava and her friends abandoned what was left of their deserts and slipped out through the side door.

'I know where we can go to be out of the way,' Libby said,

leading the way.

She took them around the side of the building and headed toward the bike sheds.

'Erm, there's always people hanging around there,' Ava commented, 'so that's probably not the best place to be for practicing magic.'

Libby didn't respond. She just carried on leading the way until they reached the bike sheds.

'There's no one here,' Willow said, looking around.

'There will be soon enough,' Ava said, 'when they all start piling out of the dining hall in a bit.'

'Good job we won't be here, then, isn't it?' Libby said as she disappeared around the back and began fighting her way past some branches which were protruding through the fence.

'Where *are* you going?' Ava asked her.

'Just follow,' Libby said.

So Ava and Willow did (with Ava getting slapped in the face by a branch for her troubles). And further along the fence, Libby slipped through a gap in the mesh. She beckoned the others to follow her and they once again did, emerging into the wooded area next to the school.

'I never knew this gap was here,' Ava said.

'Neither did I,' Libby said, 'until a few weeks ago when I saw some boys disappear around the back of here. And, of course, I had to follow and find out what they were up to, which was making themselves a base.' She pointed off into the distance to the right. 'It's over there and it's quite cool.

Must have taken them some time to put it together.'

'Is that where we're going?' Willow asked.

'No,' Libby said as she set off and led the others through the trees. 'We don't want to be disturbed and they might rock up and then things could get heated. That'd be more beef that we don't need.'

'How's your head?' Willow asked her as they all waded their way through long grass, pushing branches out of the way.

'I'm fine now,' Libby said. 'That's the last time I ever eat anything cold quickly. It felt as if someone had taken a sword made of ice and plunged it through the side of my frickin' skull.'

'Almost makes me want to try it to see what it's like,' Willow said.

'Not the smartest thing you'd ever do,' Ava said.

'That's why I used the word almost,' Willow said, smiling at her. 'I wouldn't *actually* be daft enough to do it.'

'Right, this'll do,' Libby said, pointing to a fallen tree that she could see in a good-sized clearing. They all perched themselves on it with Willow sandwiched between the two girls.

'Right, the most important thing first,' Ava said, gesturing eagerly toward Willow, 'we need to know whether that new book you've got is the real deal.'

Placing her bag down gently, Willow reached inside and pulled out the book. She looked from one girl to the other as she ran her fingers over the cover. And then she opened it at a random page, about a quarter of the way through.

'A spell to make you strong,' Libby said, leaning in to get a good look. 'Now *that* sounds interesting.'

'Says in the notes that it lasts for a short period only,' Ava added, nodding her approval. 'Up to five minutes, max. More lasting effects can be gained with a potion. It's a medium-level spell, so this should be quite doable for you, Willow.'

'Should be,' she said as she stood up, stepped away from the other two and turned to face them. 'But there's always that worry of mispronouncing a word and ending up with unexpected results. Knowing my luck I'll sprout two heads or something.'

'No you won't,' Ava said, injecting some positivity. 'You've got this. Just stay calm and you'll be fine.'

'Deep breaths,' Libby said, doing some of her own. 'Ava is right; you've got this.'

Willow took a moment to steady herself. She took one deep breath, then read the magical words, loudly and clearly: 'Fortisum Gravisia Temporalus!'

The other two looked at her expectantly …

And then Libby said, 'Well, do you feel any different?'

'Erm … no,' Willow replied. 'It might have worked and it might not.'

'There's only one way to find out,' Ava said. She looked around for something heavy that Willow could pick up, but she couldn't see anything suitable. 'How about Libby? You could grab hold of an arm and a leg and hoist her over your head like she's a barbell full of weights.'

Libby did not look impressed at this suggestion. 'Or how about Ava? She weighs more than me, so it'll be more of a challenge.'

Ava placed a hand on her chest and pretended to be insulted. 'I do *not* weigh more than you, thank you very much. What a thing to say!'

'Well, what a thing to suggest, though,' Libby said. 'As if I'm going let anybody use me like I'm a ba –'

Both of them screeched as the tree they were sitting on was slowly raised in the air. Ava looked down to her left and saw Willow's smiling face looking up at her. Libby chuckled when she realized what was happening.

'Ha-hah! I love it!' she exclaimed. 'You're making it look so easy. Move over Supergirl; there's a new superhero in town. Whoa! *Whoa* – steady on! I nearly slipped off then.'

'I think we can safely say that the book is legit,' Ava said, digging her fingernails into the bark to hold herself steady, 'so you can put us down now, Willow.'

Willow set them down gently and went to retrieve her book, which she'd left perched on top of a stump. She skimmed eagerly through the pages, her eyes wide with excitement.

'How do you feel?' Ava asked her.

'Like Supergirl,' Willow said, beaming.

'No, I don't mean that,' Ava said. 'When you did spells with that dark magic book, it took something out of you. You felt drained. Do you feel drained now? Or just ... normal?'

'I feel fine,' Willow reported, still skimming. 'Hey, there's one in here for making you faster. But like the strength one, it only lasts for a few minutes – much longer effects to be gained from a potion. Crikey, I can't wait to get my hands on that potions book.'

'So does this mean that we can safely rule out the idea that Miss Becker could be an evil witch?' Libby asked.

'Probably,' Ava answered. 'I don't think she'd have exchanged books with Willow if she were evil. She'd have just confiscated the one she wanted. I mean, she's a teacher, so she could have easily done that – with no magic needed to be used. But even if she isn't evil, there's still the memory-wiping threat to consider. What are we going to do about *that*?'

'Do we go for a pre-emptive strike or not?' Willow said, puffing her cheeks out in indecisive frustration.

'Something's just occurred to me,' Libby said. 'Miss Becker probably has friends who are witches and wizards. There'll soon twig on to what's happened and could do a spell to make her regain her memories.'

'I haven't noticed any spell in my new book for regaining memories,' Willow was keen to point out.

'Just because it's not in that book doesn't mean that it can't be done,' Libby said. 'I doubt that book covers every spell there is.'

'So what do we do then?' Ava said, getting more and more annoyed with the situation.

'Miss Becker told us that she'd sleep on it and get back to

us with a decision tomorrow,' Willow said, 'so perhaps we should do the same. Let's just all go away and mull things over, then meet up in the morning and brainstorm. What do you say?'

'Sounds good to me,' Libby said.

'But what if she makes up her mind today?' Ava said. 'What if she decides to just get it over and done with?'

'We'll just have to keep a close eye on her,' Libby said. 'If she so much as even looks at me for more than one second, I'm legging it. Thankfully we don't have any more lessons with her today, so at least that's something.'

'Do you think that's what we should do?' Ava asked Willow. 'Just hope for the best for the rest of the day?'

She was quick to reply: 'We can't think of what to do about tomorrow, so we don't have a choice. But as Libby says, if she looks at you for more than one second and starts spouting strange words, you need to vamoose. Take off like Road Runner being chased by Wile E Coyote.'

'I don't think you've got anything to worry about,' Ava said to her. 'It's me and Libby she's concerned about.'

'As I said before, she threatened to wipe my memory as well,' Willow responded.

'Only because you said that you'd tell us about everything that'd happened anyway,' Ava said.

'Which I would still do,' Willow was keen to point out.

Ava felt a gush of friendly affection for her. They hadn't known each other for long and yet Willow was prepared to take such a big risk for her and Libby. It made Ava's stomach tingle with butterflies.

'Okay,' Libby said, smiling at Willow, 'I guess we'll just have to take our chances then. All agreed?'

Ava and Willow nodded.

'And now on to the next problem,' Ava said. 'What are we going to do about Ruth and Amy?' She sported a cunning smile as she focused on Willow. 'How can we "persuade them" to leave us alone?'

'You want me to come up with a magical solution?' Willow said, looking excited at the prospect. 'But you made me promise not to use magic against them.'

'That's because you were talking about making them disappear,' Ava said. 'If you can just come up with something that doesn't involve them getting hurt or ceasing to exist ...'

'That could be something else for you to think about this evening,' Libby said to Willow. 'I'm sure there must be a spell in that book that can help us out, yeah?'

'I would think so,' Willow said, opening the book and running her finger down the table of contents.

'Don't worry about it now,' Ava said, standing up.

'You could just use the strength spell,' Libby suggested with a playful glint in her eyes. 'You could pick them up and toss them around a bit. Show them who's boss. I'm sure that'd do the trick.'

'It would also raise some eyebrows,' Ava noted. 'And they'll probably get hurt. Willow shouldn't be doing anything that'll attract attention to her (even though it would be hilarious to watch, I've got to admit). But anyway, as I just said, let's not worry about it now. Let's get back to the playground before someone notices we're missing.'

'Who would notice that we're missing?' Libby said.

'Ruth and Amy could be looking for us, for all we know,' Ava said. 'And if they can't find us anywhere, they might report this to a teacher. It's unlikely – but you never know.'

'She's got a point,' Willow agreed.

'Okay,' Libby said. 'Okey-dokey-doke!' On their way back to the hole in the fence, she added, 'I've got a feeling that this isn't the last time we sneak out here for some secret time.'

'I've got a feeling you're right,' Willow agreed.

19.

The rest of the day went okay for the girls. Ava and Libby didn't get their memories wiped by Miss Becker; although there was one hair-raising moment between lessons four and five when Ava rounded a corner in the top floor hallway and came face-to-face with her. Straightening up as if she'd just been electrocuted, Ava said hello and scurried away with life-dependent urgency. With regards to Ruth and Amy, there were the usual run-ins for the girls – the dirty looks and sneaky remarks – but no full-on confrontations.

At home time, Ava walked with her friends up the main road. They earwigged a disturbing conversation between two older boys who were ahead of them. One of them was short and tubby with a shock of frizzy blonde hair and the other one looked like a tall, thin stretched out version of him.

'It was the most disgusting thing I've *ever* seen in my life,' the tall one said, screwing his face up to emphasise just exactly how disgusted he was. 'There were loads of dried-up ones that looked like they'd been there for a *looooong* time.'

'What did the teacher say when he caught him doing it?' the tubby one said, looking more disturbed than disgusted.

'He asked him to turn his desk over. And that's when the whole class erupted. Everyone was grossed out. I mean, we all pick our noses, but I'd never wipe it on the bottom of my desk. Ah, man, I don't think I'll *ever* get that image out of my head. There must have been a hundred of them there. It reminded me of one of those connect the dots drawings.'

The tubby boy pretended to retch.

All three girls stopped at the same time and looked at each other.

'I didn't need to hear that,' Willow said.

'Me neither,' Libby said, pretending to retch as well. 'That's got to be the grossest thing I've ever heard. Whoever's done that will never live it down. I wonder who it is.'

'We'll find out soon enough,' Ava said. 'Tomorrow, at school, news of it will spread quickly. I probably won't be able to eat my dinner now.' She shuddered. 'Honestly, some people just baffle me with the things they do.'

Before going their separate ways, she reminded them to get their thinking caps on in the evening.

'Don't worry,' Willow said, looking confident, 'I'll think of some way to deal with Ruth and Amy.' She rubbed her hands together. 'I'm looking forward to this. Oh boy, am I looking forward to this!'

Libby let out an evil chuckle.

'And we need to put together a plan to deal with Miss Becker,' Ava said, not appearing quite so optimistic. 'Willow and I have got an English lesson with her tomorrow – lesson three – so that's going to be awkward and nervy.'

'One of us will have a bright spark moment,' Libby assured her. 'You'll see.'

20.

And by eight o'clock that evening, the lack of optimism was beginning to intensify for Ava. She was still clueless about what to do with regard to Miss Becker. She kept going around in circles with the options, of which there were only two, as far as she could see: either do nothing and hope for the best or get Willow to perform a pre-emptive strike. Neither option was appealing but a choice needed to be made. Collapsing on her bed and sprawling out, Ava punched the wall in frustration.

On a more positive note, her parents had returned earlier with some good news. The meeting with Mrs Fernsby had gone well and they'd persuaded her to reduce the number of detentions to just one. The bad news was that the one remaining detention was slated for Saturday. When Ava had asked her parents why she still had one to attend, they'd told her that it was because she hadn't handled the situation well. This was a fair enough assessment and justified (kind of – maybe – or *not*!). But why a *Saturday*? All Ava had managed to get from her parents with regards to this was a shrug of the shoulders from her mother and an 'Oh, well,' from her dad. Which was great – just blumin' great!

At Bedtime, Ava snuggled under her covers. In the dull but reassuring glow from her nightlight, she pulled the covers up to her chin as she concentrated on the problem of Miss Becker. She was still determined to think of something better than the crappy options that were currently open to her.

Fifteen or so minutes later – still none the wiser – Ava's eyes began to slowly close as she slipped off into a fitful sleep.

But then Ava sat up suddenly as an idea popped into her head. She couldn't prevent Miss Becker from wiping her memory (short of doing something dramatic, of course). If her teacher was truly determined to do it, then she would most likely succeed. The best thing to do, as far as Ava could see, was to forget about trying to prevent it from happening and concentrate on the aftermath.

Springing up out of bed, Ava searched through her drawers for a pen and paper. When she finally located them, she sat down at her dresser and wrote a note to herself, detailing everything that'd happened with regards to Willow and the magical books. It took her five minutes to fill a sheet of A4 and another five to decide where to hide it. The note needed to be somewhere that her mum wouldn't find it (her dad rarely ventured into her bedroom, so she didn't need to worry about him).

The best place she could think of was the secret pocket in her best jacket. This was where she put her money when she went out and didn't want to get pickpocketed. It wasn't exactly an ideal hiding place, but it would have to do.

21.

As Ava was about to leave for school, Mrs Greenwood gave her the inevitable lecture in the doorway.

'Now, I don't want you getting into any more trouble with those horrible girls,' she said, giving Ava a once over and nodding her approval. 'If they say anything nasty to you, just tell a teacher. If they start pushing you around, just tell a teacher. If they cause any sorts of problems at all ...'

'Tell a teacher,' Ava said, finishing the sentence for her. 'Yeah, all right, I get it.'

Cocking her head slightly to one side, Mrs Greenwood gave her a look which suggested she was not to be messed with this morning. 'You should just thank yourself lucky that me and your father went to the school and talked to your headmistress. You were facing three detentions and we've got that down to just one, so a little appreciation would be nice. And don't you go getting all sulky because you think you don't deserve that one detention, because you do. You handled things poorly ...'

'Yes, I know I did,' Ava said, interrupting her again. 'I'm not being sulky or complaining. And, believe me, I really do appreciate what you and Dad have done. But why have I got a detention on a *Saturday*? It could easily have been arranged for a weekday, don't you think?'

'You need to ask your headmistress. I'm sure she'll be able to tell you. And just so you know, your father was quite worried about you this morning before he left for work. He wanted to speak to you, but he had to go early so he could beat the traffic.'

Good old Dad, Ava thought. If he were there now, she'd have given him a big hug.

Mrs Greenwood gave her daughter one final check-over and another nod of approval. 'Right, well, get yourself gone then – or you'll be late.'

Ava did not need prompting twice. She raised her hand and set off for school.

22.

Ava met up with Libby and Willow at the school gates. Eager to talk to them, she coaxed them to one side so they could be away from potential earwiggers.

'So …' Ava said, eyeing her friends expectantly, 'what have you been able to come up with? What are we going to do about Miss Becker?'

A shrug from Willow was answer enough.

Libby was somber. 'I couldn't think of anything,' she

replied. 'Absolutely blumin' nothing. I went to bed early and laid there for hours, thinking things through – and I couldn't think of a thing. Next thing I knew, my alarm clock was going off and it was time to get up. I was so angry with myself. And I still am.'

'I couldn't think of anything either,' Ava admitted. 'The best I've been able to think of is to write myself a note, detailing everything that's happened.' She explained where she'd hidden it and the reason why. 'It should be safe there and I'll eventually find it when I get some pocket money.'

'What if your mum decides that today is the day that your jacket needs a wash?' Willow said.

'That's unlikely,' Ava said. 'She tends to wash clothes at the weekend. And she washed my jacket a few weeks ago.'

'Damn, why couldn't I think of that,' Libby said, annoyed with herself. 'Such a simple idea, but it's an effective backup if things go badly. The note is a great idea, Ava. I don't feel quite so scared now. Hey, should I write one to myself and hide it somewhere? In my bag, yeah? In one of my books? Just in case yours gets washed or discovered.'

'Sure,' Ava said. 'It can't hurt.'

'What about me?' Willow asked. 'Should I write one?'

'Again,' Ava said, 'it can't hurt. But I am eager to know if you've thought of a way to deal with Ruth and Amy. Tell me you've found something good in that amazing book of yours ...'

A broad, toothy grin spread slowly across Willow's face. 'Oh yes,' she said, nodding with some swag, 'I've found something, all right.' She pulled the other two closer and filled them in.

'*Ooooooh!*' Libby said, her mouth forming an O of surprise. 'That's naughty – but I like it! I like it a *lot!*'

Ava liked it too. 'If that doesn't do the trick, then I don't know what will.'

'It'll do the trick,' Willow assured her. 'And I only need to do it to Ruth, because I don't think Amy will be a problem after we've dealt with her friend. But you did make me promise that I wouldn't use magic against the idiots, though, remember? Am I excused from that promise now?'

'Yes!' Ava and Libby said in unison.

'Well, you're not talking about making anyone disappear this time,' Libby said, 'so that's why you're getting the nod.'

'As if I would have done such a thing anyway,' Willow said with a naughty twinkle in her eyes.

All three of them took a moment to lap up the misfortune that would soon befall the girl who'd been making their lives hell.

The joyous mood soon evaporated, however, when Ava reminded her friends about the other problem they were facing. 'English with Miss Becker will be a nervy hour,' she said. 'I'm going to have one eye on her and one on the clock.'

Willow said, 'I hope she's remembered to bring in the potions book and wand she promised me. I can't *wait* to get my hands on those! Roll on lesson three!'

'I wish I could share your enthusiasm about the day ahead,' Ava said.

'Me too,' Libby added.

'I'm sure you pair will be fine,' Willow assured them. 'Miss Becker will have seen sense and come to the right decision.'

'What have you got first?' Libby asked her.

'Science with Miss Williams. She's quickly becoming my fav teacher. Why can't they all be as nice and helpful as her? I don't need to worry about Ruth and Amy until lesson four. I've got computer studies with them, so that's going to be fun. Well, I say I don't need to worry about them, but they could try and duff me up during one of the breaks. I'll do my best to avoid them.'

'Just concentrate on what you've got planned for Ruth and that'll get you through,' Ava said. 'And, yeah, you're right about Miss Williams; she's one of my favorites.'

'If all the teachers were like her I'd be a lot more enthusiastic about coming to school,' Libby said.

The bell sounded and Mr Shaw appeared from a side door, bustling about, struggling to get everyone inside the building.

'We need to tune Ruth and Amy out of our day and concentrate on the biggest threat,' Ava said. 'Miss Becker.'

'I'll get my note written in my first lesson and slip it inside my pencil case,' Libby said.

'I'll do the same,' Willow added. 'Hey, have you pair still got detention this afternoon?'

'Nope – not today,' Libby said. 'Mrs Fernsby called my parents yesterday afternoon and told them that the Thursday and Friday ones had been quashed. That's the good news. The bad news is that the Saturday one still stands.'

'Same for me,' Ava said, rolling her eyes.

'Oh well, two out of three cancelled is still a result, I'd say,' Willows put in.

'Yeah, but ... a Saturday, though,' Ava said. 'I mean ...'

'Erm, I think we better move,' Libby said. 'Mr Shaw is gawking at us and looking pretty stressed.'

The three girls scurried across the playground to the main entrance.

In the foyer, they stepped to the side so they would be out of the way of the stream of kids that was now coming through the door.

'Part of me wants to avoid Miss Becker at all costs,' Libby said, 'and another part of me just wants to run into her and get it over and done with. But is there even any point in trying to avoid her? We need to know what her decision is and we won't be able to avoid her for long anyway. It's a shame that we don't know where she is now so that we can go and have it out with her straight away. Any ideas?'

'Probably in the staff room,' Ava said. 'I don't fancy going there and knocking on the door. Whoever answers will ask us why we're not in registration. And we'll be late for that if we stand here too long. We just need to be patient and remember that we do have a backup plan in place now if it comes to the worst.'

'But what if Miss Becker anticipates that we've got a backup plan?' Libby said. 'What if she uses a spell on us that forces us to tell her about it? Or it could even be a potion that she'll try to slip into our drinks at lunchtime. I don't think our note plan is going to work if she's decided to do the dirty on us.'

Ava didn't know what to say to this. She just stood there in shocked silence, frantically running things through in her head.

'Ok, you pair just need to calm down,' Willow said. 'It's too late to start worrying about things like that. And you need to stop assuming the worst. I don't think that she'll be wiping any memories, so just take a chill pill and relax.'

Take a chill pill and relax? Ava thought. *Are you for real?*

But she took a deep breath anyway in an attempt to at least appear to be trying to compose herself.

'What if I'm right, though?' Libby said, biting down on her bottom lip in worry. 'What if she does use a spell or potion on us to make us tell the tru –'

Ava told her to be quiet, then focused her attention on Willow. 'Can you please check if there's anything in your books to see if such a spell or potion exists and whether it can be countered?'

'Okay,' she said, reaching into her bag.

'No, not now,' Ava said, 'there isn't enough time. Just as soon as you get a chance.'

'Well, that's realistically going to be at break time,' Willow said.

'We only have one lesson to get through to get to that,' Libby noted. 'I think we can make it to then.'

The stream of kids coming through the foyer had now tapered off to a trickle.

Ava was about to suggest that the three of them get moving when Mr Shaw appeared in the doorway and asked them to vacate the area.

The girls scurried through the inner doorway and down the corridor. They looked over their shoulders in dismay to see that he was following them.

'We're not going to be able to talk about this anymore now,' Ava said, 'so let's just get to our registrations.'

An agreement was made that this was the best course of action.

23.

As first lessons go, biology wasn't a bad start to the day as far as Ava was concerned. But she couldn't concentrate on anything she was being taught. All she could think about were the problems she and her friends were facing and how to deal with them. Inevitably, the teacher picked up on this and asked Ava if anything was troubling her. *Oh, where do I begin!* Ava thought. But she told the teacher that she was fine and that nothing was playing on her mind at all. This was so far removed from the truth that Ava almost let out a chuckle of despair. She managed to keep herself composed, however, and made an effort to appear more with it for the rest of the lesson.

About halfway through, Ava felt overcome by an urgent

need for the toilet. At first, she was determined to hold her bladder. She'd never had to ask to go during a lesson before and she was determined that this would not be the first time. But after about five to ten minutes of discomfort, the need to go became overwhelming and Ava was faced with a difficult choice: try to hold out for the remainder of the lesson or succumb to the inevitable. She did not fancy peeing herself in front of the rest of the class, so she raised her hand and asked the question.

'Did you not go before school?' Mrs Brown asked her irritably.

'No,' Ava replied, 'because I didn't need to go then.'

This elicited a few chuckles of laughter, which were silenced immediately by icy stares from Mrs Brown.

She turned her attention back to Ava. 'Don't drag your heels,' she snapped. 'Make it quick!'

Ava scurried out of the classroom with an uncomfortable feeling in the pit of her stomach, which had nothing to do with her desperation to pee. She did not like this. She did *not* like this one bit. *And I haven't even had anything to drink today*, she thought dismally. This made her even more suspicious of her sudden desperation to empty her bladder. The situation stunk of a trap. But all she could do was go along with it. Fleeing the school was the only other option and that seemed extreme (and would take some explaining). *What if it isn't a trap? What if my bladder is just playing me up?* Ava thought.

Mrs Brown's words replayed in her head: 'Make it quick!'

Ava got moving. She headed for the nearest toilet, which was at the end of the corridor. But as she was passing the southern stairwell she changed her mind and nipped down to the first floor. If Miss Becker was waiting for her in a toilet, it would surely be the one closest to the biology room. That was the logic behind Ava's choice.

The door creaked open as she entered. The only sound to be heard in here was that of a dripping tap. Ava wanted to make sure there was no one else in the room, so she checked the cubicles one after another. Satisfied that she was on her own, she locked herself in the one at the end and began to do her business. As soon as she parked her bottom down on the icy-cold seat, however, the door creaked open – and someone else entered.

Who in the blue heck is that? Ava thought. She sat motionless as she listened to the tiptap of approaching footsteps. She heard cubicle doors being pushed open and the sound of them slowly shutting as the person moved closer to her. Ava waited ... and then the door rattled on its hinges as someone – *please don't let it be Miss Becker!* – attempted to open it. Ava was about to lower herself down in an attempt to see beneath the gap at the bottom of the door when a familiar voice spoke up:

'Hello? Who's in there?'

'Libby!' Ava said, her voice echoing off the tiled walls. Quickly pulling up her underwear and skirt, Ava opened the door and greeted her friend with a big smile. 'I thought you were ...'

'Miss Becker.' Libby said. 'And, don't tell me, you're here because you had an overwhelming need to go for a pee, right?'

Ava nodded. 'We need to get out of here. And we need to get out of here *now*.'

Before either of them could move, however, the door creaked open and Miss Becker entered the room. The door creaked slowly shut behind her.

'I'm sorry it's come to this,' she said as she produced a wand from beneath her florally decorated top, 'but what needs to be done, needs to be done.'

'It doesn't need to be done, though,' Ava said. 'We won't blab. We're not like that. We can be trusted!'

'Yeah, we can be trusted!' Libby added.

'For what it's worth, I'm ninety-eight percent sure that you're right,' Miss Becker said. 'But that's not the only reason for me wanting to erase your recent memories. And now, before I do the honors, I'd just like to thank you for finding a copy of the Shadowbound for me. You have no idea how long I've been searching for one and I will be forever grateful to you for bringing it into my possession. I will now be able to realize my *true* potential as a witch.'

'You were always going to erase our memories, weren't you?' Ava said.

'Yes,' Miss Becker confirmed.

'So why didn't you just do it yesterday when Willow handed you that evil book?' Ava said. 'Why give us false hope and a night of worries when none of it was needed?'

'There are a few reasons,' Miss Becker said. 'Firstly, I wasn't fully aware of what Willow was capable of, magic-wise. Yes, I was aware that she's a novice, but I didn't know which spells she knew and thus how much of a threat she would be. I still don't know. Secondly, I wanted a bit of time to think about how I was going to handle the situation with regard to her. I needed to mull over things and formulate the best course of action.'

'Shall we just rush her?' Libby whispered in Ava's ear. 'We might be able to get to her before she says the words.'

'The acoustics are very good in here,' Miss Becker said, 'so I just heard every word of your suggestion. Just so you're aware. And, no, you won't get to me in time. Just so you're aware of that, too.'

'Does this mean that Willow won't be getting the wand and potions book that you promised her?' Libby said. 'She's going to be *very* disappointed if that's the case.'

'I'll be dealing with her in due course,' Miss Becker replied. She raised her wand and pointed it at Ava. 'Don't worry, this will be painless and the effects instantaneous ...'

'Hang on!' Ava said, splaying her hands out in a warding-off gesture. 'Someone could burst through that door at any second: another student, or a teacher, wondering where we are. And Willow will know what you've done to us. She'll restore our memories by telling us everything. You know she will!'

'I've planned for any contingencies that you lot will have concocted,' Miss Becker said with a confident smile. 'And as far as Willow goes, as I just stated, I'll deal with her soon enough. The power of suggestive thought can be used for much more than making someone think they need to relieve their bladder. I think you can guess how I'll convince her that this is for the best. If the spell doesn't work, there's a potion – which will be much more effective – to consider. A little drop in her drink will do the trick.'

'Do you know what,' Libby said, glaring at her, 'I've always thought that you were a miserable old trout, but I never had you down as being downright evil.'

'As if I care what you think of me,' Miss Becker said, raising her wand again.

'No wait ... hang on!' Ava said, still trying to stall her.

The door creaked open and Willow appeared behind Miss Becker, who pivoted quickly around to see who'd entered.

'Rigidio Maximus!' Willow said, focusing all her attention on the teacher.

For a moment there was silence in the room. Nobody moved or said anything. The only sound that could be heard was from the tap:

... drip ... drip ... drip ...

It was Ava who moved first. Taking tentative steps forward, she stood in front of Miss Becker and waved a hand in front of her eyes. The teacher didn't react in any way. She just stood there like a statue, her eyes unblinking, her wand held out and ready, a look of shock on her face.

'I'll take that, thank you very much,' Willow said, snatching it from her. 'Oh Well, at least I got the wand I wanted. Now, how am I going to get my hands on that potions book I still need? Hmmmm?'

'How did you know we were here?' Libby asked her.

'I saw you walking past my classroom door and guessed that something must be going down,' Willow said. 'So I got thinking, quickly put two and two together, then told the teacher that I was desperate for the toilet. I tried to follow you, but by the time I got in the corridor, you'd already disappeared from view. I looked around for a bit, then put two and two together again and figured out what might be going on. I checked two other toilets before finally finding you. That's why it took me so long to get here.'

'I'm just glad that you *did* find us,' Libby said, moving in front of Miss Becker and looking at her through slitted eyes, 'otherwise we'd have had our memories wiped by this nasty piece of work here. She had no intention of not doing it. The spell she used to get us here was something to do with suggestive power and that's what she was going to use on you after she'd dealt with us. She'd have brainwashed you into thinking whatever she wanted. She was looking quite smarmy before you turned up, Willow. But she's not looking so smarmy now.'

Libby stepped back and gestured for Willow to take her place, which she did.

'So what are we going to do with her?' Ava said. 'We can't just leave her like that. How long does the freeze spell last? And can she hear what we're saying?'

'She can hear every word,' Willow said, looking Miss

Becker dead in the eyes. 'And it lasts long enough for what I've got planned. *Eww!*' Willow pulled a face, disgusted. 'Did you clean your teeth this morning, love? Your breath stinks!'

Ava and Libby chuckled, then went to stand by the door.

Then Ava said, 'Whatever you've got planned, you need to get on with it. Anyone could walk through this door and then we'll have some real explaining to do.'

Willow took a few steps back and said, 'Ah, that's better. I can breathe now.' She inhaled and exhaled to emphasize the point – and then added, 'Ever since you gave me that book of spells, I've been studying it and memorizing as many as I can. But the memory wipe is the one I've been most keen to remember, though. For obvious reasons. Obviously I haven't had a chance to practice it on anyone else, so I might get this right – and I might get it wrong. But I'll give it a good go, I can assure you of that.' Willow raised the wand and then moved to be with her friends as she was saying the magical words …

'Oblivious Recallaria Tempris!' She repeated this three times.

Willow lowered the wand. And then all that could be heard again was the sound of the dripping tap.

Ava asked her to clarify exactly what she'd done.

Willow beckoned her and Libby to go through the door, so they all piled into the corridor.

As they made their way to the nearest stairwell, springing along excitedly, Willow tucked the wand beneath her top and said, 'I've made her forget that she's a witch. And I've also erased all her memories from the last few days, so that "should" solve our problems. What do you think?'

Libby stopped dead and pointed to something in front of them. 'We're about to be in trouble,' she said. 'That what's I think.'

Ahead of them, at the bottom of the stairwell, two teachers had just emerged and were now making their way briskly toward the girls. They looked worried and angry.

Off the top of her head, Ava could not think of any plausible explanation as to why all three of them were together. And neither could Libby and Willow, judging by their blank expressions.

24.

At break time, the girls hung out in their usual place in the far corner of the playground. Overhead, a mass of dark grey clouds was edging in from the east. The air felt heavy and thick with the promise of rain. Ava and the others hoped that it would hold off for another fifteen minutes.

'I passed Miss Becker in the foyer on the way out here and she said hello to me,' Willow told the other two.

'Did she do anything to make you feel suspicious? Did she give you any sly looks?'

'No,' Willow replied, 'not that I noticed.'

'So it's definitely worked then,' Libby said.

'It looks that way,' Willow said. 'Unless she's just pretending to be oblivious. The safest thing would be to assume the worst and be on guard all the time until we can be sure, one way or another.'

'So what will have happened with her when that freeze spell wore off?' Ava asked her. 'Did she just un-freeze and go back to what she'd been doing, teaching her class?'

'She'll have been disoriented at first because she'll have no recollection of how she came to be in that toilet,' Willow replied. 'And then, yeah, she'll have gone back to the class once she got herself together and realized where she should have been.'

'She still has the Shadowbound,' Libby said. 'So what are we going to do about that? And what will she have made of it when she found it in her bag or wherever she's been keeping it?'

'She might not have come across it yet,' Ava said. 'Two of us could try distracting her while the other searches through her stuff? Her desk and bag, yeah?'

'And if we get caught doing that,' Willow said, 'what will our excuse be?'

'We'd just have to make sure we don't get caught,' Ava replied.

'And if we can't find it, what then?' Willow said. 'Do we find out where she lives and burglarize her house? I think we'd get a bit more than a detention if we were caught doing *that*! And can you imagine having to explain it to our parents?' She shuddered at the idea. 'I don't even want to think about how my mum would react. The word nuclear comes to mind.'

'My dad would explode,' Libby said.

'I've just thought of a problem,' Ava said, worried. 'What if Miss Becker's got friends who know she's a witch? What if they're magical as well? They'll know something's wrong and figure out what's happened. They'll tell her and then probably restore her memories. Is that possible, Willow? Did you notice anything in either of the books about that?'

Willow nodded. 'I noticed spells for restoring memories in both of the books, so, yeah, it's possible.'

Ava puffed out her cheeks in exasperation. 'Crikey, talk about solve one problem and create a load more.'

After a moment of contemplative silence, Libby veered the conversation in a different direction. 'Hey, I've found out who the boy is that's been putting bogies under his desk. It's a year 8: Liam Watson. Do either of you know who he is?'

Willow shook her head. 'I don't even know many people in my own year yet, never mind another.'

'I'll probably know him by sight rather than by name,' Ava said.

'He's really small and skinny,' Libby said. 'Got spiky hair, beady eyes and a paper-white complexion, like a vampire.'

'Ah, yeah,' Ava said, 'I know who you mean. Loads of people are talking about him. If I were him, I wouldn't have come in today. I'd have thrown a sickie. In fact, I'd never come back to this school ever again. The shame would be too great! But then I wouldn't be stupid enough to do what he's done.'

'I know we've got problems – *big* problems,' Libby said,

'but I'd still take ours over his any day.'

'Definitely,' Willow agreed.

'Speaking of problems,' Ava said, nodding toward something on the other side of the playground, 'look who's making her way over here.'

The other two noticed what that something was and reacted accordingly.

'Oh great,' Libby said, 'like we haven't got enough on our plate at the moment.'

'And she's got her sidekick with her as well,' Willow said. 'No surprise there.'

'So has this become your spot then?' Ruth said as she approached with Amy. 'I hope we're not invading your territory.'

'It's not our territory,' Libby said.

'Oh well, we'll come and sit here every break time then,' Amy said, 'if that's all right?'

'Yeah, that's fine by us,' Ava said.

Ruth and Amy did not look happy with this response. Ava figured that they'd expected some sort of protest and were peeved at not getting it.

'Don't forget that we've got detention this afternoon,' Ruth said to Ava and Libby.

'You have,' Ava replied. 'We haven't.'

'What?' Ruth said, shocked. 'How come?'

'Their parents talked to our headmistress yesterday,' Willow said with a smug smile touching her lips, 'and they convinced her to reduce the three detentions down to only one.'

'*What?*' Ruth said, even more shocked. She glared at Ava and Libby. 'You pair only have one detention now?'

'Yep,' Libby confirmed. 'It's the Saturday one, though, if that makes you feel any better.'

The look on Ruth's face suggested that it didn't. 'That's not fair,' she said. 'I'm going to complain to Mrs Fernsby about this.'

'I don't think that'll help,' Libby said.

'Perhaps you should convince your parents to pay Mrs Fernsby a visit,' Ava said, lapping up Ruth and Amy's annoyance. 'It worked out well for me.'

'I wouldn't look too pleased about this,' Amy warned her. 'You'll have that smile wiped off your face soon enough.'

'I'm not even smiling,' Ava said.

'No,' Amy said, 'but you want to, though, don't you?'

Yes, Ava thought, *I very much do*. But she denied the accusation, just to keep the peace.

'We don't want any trouble,' Willow said.

Amy looked her up and down and said, 'Isn't it about time you got a new uniform? Honestly, I've seen tramps dressed better than you. Can't your parents afford new clothes? We can arrange a whip-round for you if you like? Anything to help!'

Willow did not reply. She just stared at her with her lips pursed tightly together.

And that's when it began raining. A few fat splodges dropped at first – and then the heavens opened up and it threw it down.

This got everyone moving. Along with all the other kids in the playground, they made for the entrance as quickly as they could. The doorway soon became crammed with bodies, however, causing a bottleneck.

'Around the side,' Ava suggested, leading the way.

The others followed – including Ruth and Amy.

As they neared the side entrance, Amy pushed past Ava so she could be first inside and this nearly caused another argument. Ava came very close to telling her what she thought of her, but she decided to bite down on her lip instead. Hard enough to draw blood.

'I'm going to tell my parents about you only having one detention now,' Ruth said to Amy, 'and they'll pay a visit to the school, just like yours did.'

'That's not going to stop you from having one this evening, though, is it?' Willow said.

'No, it won't,' Ruth admitted with water dripping down her face. 'But I wouldn't look so smug about that. You'll get yours.' She marked all three girls in turn with a nasty stare. 'All of you will.'

As they were walking away, Amy added, 'Have a nice day, now, won't you! Don't go tripping over and breaking a leg or anything, 'cause that'd be a shame, wouldn't it?'

The bell sounded to end break time.

After they'd gone, Libby said, 'Brilliant! They've now got it in for us because our parents managed to get some detentions cancelled.'

'Like they didn't have it in for us anyway,' Willow said. 'Maybe looking smug wasn't such a smart thing to do, but I just couldn't help myself. Thinking about what I've got planned for Ruth makes me want to smile smugly all day.' She smiled smugly.

'I can't blame you for that,' Libby said. 'But, yeah, it certainly ticked her off.' She looked down at herself. 'Look at me, I'm soaked! We all are. Is there a spell to dry people quickly, Willow? That would be a really useful one to know right now if there is?'

'I'm not aware of one,' Libby said. 'And I haven't got time to look through the book.'

'Never mind being wet,' Ava said, 'we've got bigger things to worry about than that. What are we going to do about Miss Becker? Even if she does have friends who can restore her memories, we still need to get that book back from her. That's all we should concentrate on for now. Agreed?'

'Agreed,' Libby said.

'Yep – agreed,' Willow said. Her face darkened as something occurred to her. 'And I'll need to make her give the book to me. We can't just take it.'

'Why?' Ava said – and then she twigged. 'Ah, I get it – oh damn!'

Libby hadn't got it yet – and then she did. 'But you'll be okay because you've got the new book, yeah?' she asked Willow. 'You'll be able to resist any temptation, right?'

'I will,' she assured her. But there wasn't as much conviction in her voice as Ava would like to have heard.

'Is there no other way?' Libby said.

'No, I don't think there is,' Willow said ominously. 'We've just got to hope that there's a persuasion spell in my book. I'll have a crafty look through in my next lesson. I think there will be – probably.'

Ava put a hand on her arm. 'You can do this. You're strong enough now. And we'll decide what to do with the book when we get it back.'

Willow held her chin up high and then nodded. 'I'll hang back after the lesson and do the spell after everyone else has gone (assuming that it's in the book, of course). Damn, I wish I had time to look through now; I *really* want to know!'

'No time for that,' Libby said.

'We need to get moving,' Ava said. 'I don't want to be late for another lesson. It's getting to be a habit.'

25.

Ava couldn't concentrate in her next lesson because she was too busy worrying about what would happen with Miss Becker. She stared vacantly ahead, lost in her thoughts …

Until the teacher asked her what she was doing.

Ava noticed that everyone, including the teacher, was staring at her.

'Are you planning on doing any work today?' he asked her.

'Oh, yes – *yes*,' she replied.

She put her head down and got on with her work.

26.

When Ava arrived at her next class, she pulled Willow to one side in the corridor and said, 'Any luck?'

Willow nodded. 'We're good to go.'

Ava said, 'After everyone has left the room at the end, I'll stand outside the door to make sure no one bursts in on you while you're doing the spell, okay?'

'Okay.'

They knuckle-bumped each other.

'It's nice to see that you're happy about something,' a familiar voice said, 'but there's no need for you to be loitering in the corridor.'

The girls turned to see Miss Becker hurrying toward them, carrying a bag. She stopped by the doorway and gestured for them to pass over the threshold, which they did without hesitation.

Miss Becker did nothing during the lesson to suggest that the memory wipe spell used by Willow had been anything but successful. And when the bell rang at the end, both girls looked at each other and nodded.

Ava and Willow began packing their things away slowly as the other students left the room.

Looking up from her desk, Miss Becker marked both of them with curious stares. 'You do realize it's dinner time, right? You don't usually hang around when it's dinner time.'

'Yes,' Ava said as she made her way to the door and disappeared through it before she could be quizzed some more.

She stood to one side and watched some students who were hanging around further down the corridor, larking about and giggling.

Then the door clicked shut and Ava wondered who'd closed it. She resisted any temptation to peer through the glass as she continued to keep an eye out. The kids who'd been larking about were now moving away, the sound of their laughter fading as they disappeared down the stairwell.

A few minutes later, Willow emerged looking kind of pleased with herself.

'I take it you got it,' Ava said.

'I have,' she confirmed, tapping her bag. 'The spell worked a treat. It was locked in the bottom drawer of her desk.'

Ava couldn't resist another fist bump with her.

27.

By the time Willow and Ava reached the dinner hall, Libby was already tucking into her food in the far corner of the room. Fish, chips and mushy peas looked to be the best on offer, so that's what the girls opted for – along with a drink of orange juice and a slice of chocolate sponge cake for afters. Yummy.

'We have the book,' Ava said as she and Willow plonked their trays down and seated themselves across from Libby, 'so now all we need to worry about is the possibility of someone restoring her memory.'

Willow took a big gulp of her drink and then said, 'As we said before, there's nothing we can do where that's concerned. We're just going to have to wait and see – and be on our guard. If she does get her memory restored, she'll want that book back and may go to extremes to get it.'

'It's such a shame that we can't just hide it,' Libby said.

'But we can hide it – kind of,' Ava said. 'Miss Becker isn't the owner now, remember? Which means that she won't be able to track it down using whatever connection she had with it. She'd have to use her instincts and intelligence to figure it out. The problem that we've got is that we need someone to buy the book so that it no longer belongs to Willow. And the only way that's going to happen is by giving it to a shop. But I don't think it should be the Book Cove. That's too obvious. Another bookshop? One further away?'

'There's one in Harwich,' Libby said, 'which is about three miles away. Is that far enough?'

'Not really,' Ava said. 'The further away, the better.'

'We'd have to catch a bus or something,' Libby said.

'I'm pretty sure Miss Becker will check every secondhand book shop in the county if her memory gets restored,' Libby said, 'so all you'll be doing is delaying the inevitable. Unless someone buys it before she does, which is unlikely.'

'So what do you suggest?' Ava asked her.

'One of us needs to take it a long way away,' Libby said. 'Down south, maybe? Or up north?'

'That would involve an expensive coach ride,' Willow stated. Her mouth turned down at the corners as she thought of another problem. 'Last night, when I was looking through my book, I noticed a spell for making people tell the truth. What's to stop Miss Becker from using it to get any info out of us that she needs?'

Ava gritted her teeth in frustration. 'And I don't suppose there's any counter spell, is there?'

'Of course there won't be,' Libby said.

'I haven't noticed one,' Willow said.

'So we may as well just take it back to the Book Cove then,' Libby said.

'No, not there,' Ava said. 'Mr Grimes will start quizzing us about that non-existent twenty-pound note. He'll have all sorts of awkward questions for us; especially if he's talked to his friend, which he probably has by now.'

'The one in Harwich then?' Libby said.

'Yeah,' Ava said. 'Can we all agree on that?'

Willow nodded. 'Yep.'

'Yup,' Libby said. 'Tomorrow, after school. It's easy to find because it's on the main road that goes through the town. We'll just have to hope that it's open when we get there. Most shops shut at five, so we should be okay if that's the case. I've only been in there once, but I remember where it is.'

'And what about the magic shop?' Ava said. 'Will we have time to pull that in as well? I can't wait to go in and look around.'

'Me, too!' Willow said, spooning mushy peas excitedly into her mouth. 'We could go on our bikes. What do you say? Have you pair got bikes?'

Libby nodded. 'Yep, we've got bikes. And I'm defo up for it! We'll have to be quick, though, as we'll have to go home, get our bikes and let our parents know what we're doing (not mentioning the magic shop bit, of course). We'll just have to hope the magic shop is open till at least five as well.'

Willow went from looking excited to quite downbeat in the blink of an eye. 'I can only go in to look around, though,' she stated, 'because I don't have any money to spend.'

Ava looked at Libby. 'Have you got any dosh to spare?'

'Not really. I can ask my mum for an advance on my pocket money. Whether or not she says yes will depend on her mood. And even then, it'll only be a fiver. You can't buy much for a fiver.'

'Okay, well, that'd be better than nothing,' Ava said. 'I've still got some birthday money that I haven't spent yet …'

'Err, no!' Willow said, objecting animatedly. 'There's *no way* that I'm letting you spend your birthday money on me. Not happening!'

'It's not a problem,' Ava assured her. 'When I spend that money, I'll do it to make me happy. Getting you a potions book will make me happy. Libby and I will be able to help you make those potions if you'll let us? And if you don't want to buy a potions book, then that's fine as well. Get whatever you want and I'll still be excited. And it'll be money well spent, as far as I'm concerned.'

'Just exactly how much birthday money are we talking about here?' Libby asked.

'Fifty pounds.'

'Fifty quid!' Willow exclaimed. 'No way are you spending that on …'

Ava put a hand over Willow's mouth and said, 'Let's just go and see what they've got and then play it from there, yeah?'

Willow looked wide-eyed at her friend and then nodded. Ava removed her hand.

Willow stiffened in her chair as she looked across the hall toward the food queue. 'Uh-oh, our favorite people in the world have just entered the room.'

Ava turned to see Ruth and Amy glaring from the queue.

'Anyone up for a speed-eating contest?' Libby suggested.

'You're already halfway through your meal,' Ava noted, 'so you'll win.'

'I think she's just suggesting that we get our food in our bellies as quickly as possible so we can get out of here,' Willow said.

'That's *exactly* what I'm suggesting,' Libby said.

All three tucked into their food and had made it disappear by the time the bullies had been served.

'I'm going to get indigestion from this,' Ava said as she gulped down the remainder of her drink.

She got up and the others followed her out of the side door.

'Where can we go where *they* won't find us?' Willow said.

'I know,' Libby said as she took off and led them through the hole in the fence behind the bike sheds.

They found the large tree trunk that they'd sat on before and stayed there for the rest of the break, talking about this and that. Willow showed the wand to the other two and they each took a turn at holding it and pretending to cast spells with it. And they all laughed long and hard when they got on to the subject of what they'd got planned for Ruth.

'I just wish I could be there to see it,' Libby said.

28.

Lesson five couldn't come quickly enough, as far as Ava was concerned. She met up with Willow in the second-floor corridor and then raced to their next lesson as if their lives depended on it. The plan was for them to be the first to arrive at the classroom, but, unfortunately, someone had beaten them to it. As they burst through the door, they were disappointed to see that Sophie "the swat" Wilkes was already sitting at her desk near the front.

'Damn,' Ava whispered, 'I should have known that *she'd* be here before us.'

'Can you distract her while I do the spell?' Willow whispered back.

Sophie was eyeing them suspiciously, no doubt wondering why she was the focus of attention.

Ava went to deal with her, positioning herself so she was blocking Sophie's view of Willow.

'Hey, how's it going?' Ava said, looming over the smartest girl in the school. 'I just wondered if you'd be able to help me with some maths homework that I'm struggling with. It's to do with trigonometry. I bet you know alllll about that, yeah? I figured that if I'm going to ask someone then it should be the cleverest person I know.'

Ava was sure that flattery would at least get a civil response. She was wrong.

'If you want to know how to do trigonometry – or anything else, for that matter – then the best thing you can do is find a good book on the subject,' Sophie said, putting her nose in the air as she extolled her wisdom. 'If I help you then everyone will be on at me to help them, which won't be very good for me, now, will it?'

'Oh, okay,' Ava said, doing her best to look disappointed. 'So which book would you recommend?'

Sophie gave it some thought, then reeled off the titles of her top three. 'I'm sure you'll find at least one of those in the school library.'

Ava felt a hand touch her shoulder and turned to see Willow smiling at her.

'Come on, stop bothering her,' she said. 'Let's get seated before everyone else rocks up all rowdy.'

As if on cue, other students began arriving, laughing and joking amongst themselves as they spilled into the room.

Ava and Willow took their seats, then watched as Ruth arrived and gave them a dirty look as she was passing.

'Did you get it done okay?' Ava asked Willow.

'Yup,' she replied with a sly grin.

The noise of chitter-chatter in the room gradually rose as

more students showed up – until Mrs Pick finally arrived and told everyone to shut up and sit their backsides down.

'No Amy equals no backup,' Ava said to Willow, 'which is why this is the perfect lesson to do this in.'

Ruth was sitting next to a girl named Bianca, who was only friendly to her because of fear.

'She'll probably try and blame it on Bianca,' Ava said.

'Yeah, probably,' Willow agreed.

'*QUIET!*' Mrs Pick bellowed, bringing immediate silence to the room.

As the lesson progressed, Ava and Willow waited for the right moment to do what needed to be done. About ten minutes later, while Mrs Pick was scribbling on the whiteboard, Ava gave Willow a nod: the signal to get ready.

Ava turned on her seat, pointed at the far wall, and exclaimed, 'Ah! Look at the size of that spider!'

Chairs scraped across the floor and panic ensued as most of the kids on that side of the classroom moved to distance themselves from the area.

With this distraction in place, Willow was able to whisper the words to her spell without raising any eyebrows. This caused Ruth's desk to flip on its side, revealing an array of boogers on the underside: some dried and crusty, some fresh and gooey.

With the spider temporarily forgotten about, a sudden eruption of noise filled the room as everyone looked on with disgust.

'Those aren't mine!' Ruth was quick to point out. 'I

haven't done any of that!'

'*Ewww!*' one girl screeched. 'That is *gross*!' She covered her mouth in shock.

Another girl dry-retched while flapping her hands frantically.

'First we get Booger Boy and now we've got Booger Girl,' a boy in the back corner said. 'Dis-*gusssting!*'

Mrs Pick was quick to calm things down. She stormed to the back of the room, demanding to know what was going on. She caught sight of Ruth's desk and then demanded an explanation.

'I'm not the only person who sits here,' she explained. 'And I didn't do any of it.' She looked at Bianca, who responded with a vehement shake of her head.

'Don't try and pin that on me,' she said, pointing at the boogers. 'That's your desk, not mine!'

'I must admit,' Mrs Pick said, wrinkling her nose, 'this has to be the most vile thing I've ever seen in my life.'

'And it's *nothing* to do with me!' Ruth reiterated.

Not looking convinced, Mrs Pick righted the desk; then, with her fingertips barely touching the edges, she picked it up and made for the door.

Everyone moved out of her way, not wanting to be anywhere near it.

'I'll be back in a minute,' Mrs Pick said as she was leaving the room, 'and there better not be any trouble while I'm gone – otherwise you'll all be for it, I promise you.'

'As if there isn't going to be any trouble,' Willow

whispered in Ava's ear.

'Avoid eye contact with her,' she replied, doing just that. 'She'll be looking for someone to blame and we'll be the prime suspects.'

'What are you looking at!' Ruth screeched at a boy in front of her. She looked around the room, taking everyone in. 'Why are you all staring at me? Stop staring at me!' She looked as though she could burst into tears at any second. 'Who did this to me? Who put those bogies on the bottom of my desk?'

No one replied.

Everyone kept staring ...

Even Ava and Willow couldn't resist a look-see. Which was a mistake – a *big* mistake.

'You pair did it!' Ruth said, jabbing an accusatory finger at them. 'You pair have done this to set me up, haven't you? Go on, admit it, you ... you pair of losers!'

This got some sniggers of laughter from some of the kids. But it was Ruth's outraged reaction that turned the sniggers into an eruption of gut-busting laughter from nearly everyone.

And, of course, Mrs Pick returned at the worst possible moment – just as Ruth had picked up her chair and was threatened to throw it at someone's head.

'Err – what in the blue blazes do you think you're doing, young lady!' Mrs Pick said as she stood in the doorway with her hands on her hips and a shocked look on her face.

'The bully has become the bullied,' Willow whispered in

Ava's ear.

'I know,' she replied, beaming. 'Isn't it great?'

29.

At home time, Ava and Willow were waiting for Libby in the foyer by the main entrance when they overheard a conversation between two boys.

'She's never going to live that down,' one of them said.

'Her life's going to be hell from now on,' the other one said. 'And what makes it even worse is that they've got detention together this evening. Bogey Boy and Bogey Girl can compare notes on who has the best bogies and the best places to leave them – which would appear to be under desks.'

Both boys burst out laughing as they exited the building.

'She's got detention with Bogey Boy,' Willow said gleefully. 'Can this day get any better?'

Just then, Libby showed up and said, 'From the looks of you pair, I'd say that everything went well. Tell me all about it – every *juicy* detail.'

All three of them erupted into uncontrollable fits of laughter as they did indeed tell her everything.

30.

On Friday, the following day, none of the girls were surprised when Ruth didn't show up at school.

'I'd be pulling a sickie as well if I was in her position,' Ava said at break time as they crouched in the far corner of the playground. 'I wonder if she'll get any extra punishments because of what happened? They won't be able to prove that the bogies are hers, but she did pick a chair up and threaten someone with it. That's quite serious.'

Libby said, 'I overheard Amy saying that Ruth's mum is coming in on Monday to talk to Mrs Fernsby, so it'll be interesting to see what happens there. Let's hope that Ruth gets suspended.'

'Fingers crossed,' Willow said. 'It's what she deserves. I want to know who's cleaning those bogies off those desks, though. What a job that'd be!'

Ava gagged. 'Oh, please!' she said, 'enough talk about bogies. Can we change the subject, yeah?

They spotted Amy down the side of the building. She was on her own, crouched down, with her back against the wall.

'She's been very quiet today,' Libby noted with a smirk.

'That's not surprising after what happened to her one and only buddy,' Ava said, looking on. 'She's got no one to back her up, so perhaps she's learning what it's like to feel vulnerable. I almost feel sorry for her.'

'I don't,' Libby said.

'Me neither,' Willow added.

'Neither do I,' Ava said. 'That's why I used the word "almost".'

31.

At the end of the day, all three girls couldn't get home quickly enough.

Ava didn't bother to get changed. She explained to her mother about where she was going. Then she grabbed her money, got her bike from the garage and set off at a blistering pace with her hair flying out behind her.

They'd arranged to meet back at the school gates and she was the first one to show up. She didn't have to wait long, however, as the other two arrived together, all smiles and giggles. Both had bags on their backs.

'I knew you'd be first here,' Libby said as she skidded to a halt.

'Only just,' Ava replied, tipping her a wink. 'Are we all ready? Have we got everything we need?'

'Yup,' Libby said, reaching over her shoulder and tapping her bag.

'Double yup,' Willow said, motioning toward hers.

'And I managed to get the pocket money advance from my mum because she's in a good mood,' Libby stated.

Willow reached into her pocket and pulled out a handful of change. 'My dad didn't like the idea of me going to a bookstore empty-handed, so he cobbled together this lot.'

'How much?' Libby asked.

'Four pounds sixty-eight.'

'Cool,' Ava said. 'So with everything we've got, we might just be able to afford more than one thing.'

'So what are we waiting for?' Libby said, not wasting another second. '*Lezzzz gooooooo!*'

She sped off down the road. And the others followed.

32.

'Should we all go in or just one of us?' Libby said as they pulled up outside the shop and dismounted. She was red in the face and breathing heavily from the ride. They all were.

'You may as well do it,' Ava said, 'and we'll keep an eye on the bikes.'

'Let's just hope they accept it,' Libby said as she got the book out of her bag.

Ava noticed the way that Willow was eyeing it wistfully as Libby made for the door.

A bell tinkled as she entered.

And a few minutes later she emerged, empty-handed.

'Well, that was easy enough,' she said. 'I just told the man behind the counter that I didn't want it anymore and he was happy enough to accept it. Job done.'

'Thank goodness for that,' Willow said.

Ava just hoped that her friend would be able to resist the temptation to purchase it herself. *Please be strong, Willow*, she thought. *For your own sake as much as anything.*

'Come on,' Libby said, 'let's hit the road again before the woman changes her mind and tries to give it back to us. If the Mystic Magic does shut at five o'clock, we won't have much time to look around by the time we get there – unless we really get a move on.'

She set off with the others right behind her.

33.

The journey from Harwich to Wiggleswick only took twenty-five minutes and the girls were exhausted when they rocked up outside the shop, which they were glad to see was still open. They all marveled at the mural painted on the outside of the building. It depicted a scene that could have come straight out of a fairy tale: a giant white dragon was swooping down on a turreted castle with a silvery glowing moon as a backdrop.

'Told you it was awesome,' Libby said.

'Mega-cool!' Willow said, taking in every detail. 'And look at all this stuff that's in the window,' she added, pressing her nose against the glass. 'Look at those glass balls. Do you think they're crystal ones for seeing the future? And check out those cauldrons.' Some were bigger than others.

'I like those green candles,' Libby said, pointing. 'I wonder what they do.'

'Shed light on a dark situation,' Ava said sarcastically. 'Come on, let's get inside before the owner sees three weirdoes gawping through the window and decides to shut up earlier.'

'Hey, who are you calling a weirdo?' Libby said as she secured the bikes to a drainpipe then followed the other two in through the door.

Their arrival was announced by a jingling chime.

Ava inhaled deeply, taking in a musky smell of incense as she looked around with the others.

A small, plump man dressed in colorful robes appeared from the back and greeted them with a smile. 'Hello there!' he said jovially. 'How may I help you?'

'I'm looking for a good book on potions,' Willow said. 'One that's not too expensive, hopefully.'

'All of my goods are priced very reasonably,' the man informed her. He looked at Ava and Libby in a way that suggested he was weighing them up. 'And what about you two? Are you looking for anything particular?'

'Oh no!' Libby said. 'We're not the witches.' She gestured toward Willow. 'She's the magical one.'

'I see,' the man said, nodding. 'Well, let's see if I can find you a good potions book. What level of proficiency are you? Beginner? Or do you want something more … challenging?'

'I haven't made any potions yet, so I'm definitely a beginner,' Willow said.

'Right-o,' the man said, leading them to where all the books were displayed on the other side of the shop. He browsed along one of the shelves and then pulled out a book: *Potions for Beginners* by Phillip Regal. 'Now, you won't get much better than this one, in my opinion,' the man said, sifting through the pages. He handed the book to Willow. 'And I'll give you a ten per cent discount because you're a student. How does that sound?'

'Sounds good to me,' Willow said, noting the price on the back: £7.99. 'Thank you.' She did some sifting of her own. 'We'd like to have a really good look around to see everything you've got if that's all right?'

'Of course it is,' the man said. 'I don't close until five-thirty, so you've got plenty of time. My name's Reg, by the way: Reg Butler. And if you need anything, or you want any advice, just give me a holler and I'll be happy to help.'

The girls smiled at him and he left them to their browsing.

Willow sifted through the book and noted some of the potions. 'This one seems a little basic,' she said, handing it to Libby. 'I want something a little more ... in-depth,' she added as she plucked another, much thicker, book from the shelf: *Potions for the Inquisitive Mind: Beginner to Advanced* by Matilda Clutterbuck. 'Now *this* looks more like what I need.'

'I wouldn't attempt anything too tricky to start with,' Ava advised.

'And there are some pretty nifty potions in this one,' Libby said as she flicked through the pages of the other book. 'There's one here for zits. Now that could be a handy one to know in the future, don't you think? Check out some of these ingredients, though: frog's blood, snake venom, salt, primrose petals, vinegar, and pommus pus. I mean, where would you get some of those things? And what the heck is pommus pus?'

'Well, the salt's easy enough,' Ava said.

'I have an extensive stock of ingredients,' Reg called out from somewhere in the back. 'And on the rare occasions when I haven't got what you need, I can usually get it within a day or two.'

The girls exchanged a look and then Ava said, 'Okay – thanks for letting us know!' She signaled to the other girls with her hands: lower your voices.

Willow and Libby nodded.

'I'll go with this one,' Willow said after having a good browse through the thicker book. 'It's more expensive – £9.99 – but it's got a lot more potions in it. I'll put another cover on it when I get home because my dad will be eager to see what I've bought.'

'That still leaves us with nearly fifty quid to spend,' Libby noted. 'I wonder what else we can get with that? What else do you most need?' she asked Willow.

'Well, thanks to you know who, I don't need a wand,' Willow said. She smiled mischievously as she produced it from her bag and then stowed it back away. 'That's saved me some money. I'd still like to look at the wands, though. I spied some when I was looking through the window. Let's take a look-see.' She led the way.

The shelf they were displayed on was crammed from one side to the other with them, each one individually priced. Some were made from willow, some oak, some ash. Some were quite long and some were shorter.

'Check out this one with a lightning bolt down the side of it,' Libby said, picking it up and admiring it. 'And check out the price, too: £350. Damn! We'll probably have left school by the time we've got enough money together to buy it.'

'The cheaper ones are down this end,' Willow said, eyeing up a basic-looking one, which had a rough texture along most of its shaft. 'The least expensive is £30. Can't imagine I'll be able to do much with that!'

'Even a cheap wand can make all the difference when attempting to cast a particularly tricky spell,' Reg said, once again chirping in from the other side of the shop.

He then made the girls jump a few seconds later when he suddenly appeared next to Ava, as though he'd somehow teleported there, which Ava suspected could well have been the case.

'I'd opt for something low-end to mid-range if I were you,' he advised Willow. 'An expensive wand is a powerful one and can be a bit of a handful for a beginner.'

'Oh, I've actually got one,' she responded. 'I'm just browsing to see what you have because I might want a different one in the future.'

Reg nodded. 'Fair enough.'

'Can I try any of them out?' Willow asked. 'Perhaps the one with the lightning bolt down the side?'

'Afraid not,' Reg said with a swift shake of his head. 'I wouldn't want you practicing in my shop, for obvious reasons. And I can't allow you to leave here so you can practice somewhere else (again, for obvious reasons). I'm sure you'll be interested to know, however, that I do offer very reasonable trade-in prices. Something to bear in mind for the future.'

'I will certainly remember that,' Willow said brightly.

'Is there anything else I can help you with?' Reg asked.

'I'd like to check out the broomsticks,' Willow said, 'so I can get an idea of the prices.'

'Okey-dokey,' Reg said, shuffling off, leading the way.

The girls followed him into a room at the back, which was dedicated to displaying nothing but broomsticks. As with the wands, they were set out from the cheapest to the most expensive.

Ava noticed the price of one of the more expensive ones: £425. 'Well, you're not going to be getting this one anytime soon,' she said to Willow and then immediately regretted it when she saw the disappointment on her friend's face. 'But that's not to say that you won't be able to afford one of the cheaper ones.'

'Fifty pounds is the least expensive one that I do,' Reg said. 'It's a bit slow, but it'll get you up and about. It's been a long time since I've ridden one,' he added wistfully. 'Not sure I'd fancy it at my age now. Ay, I'd probably fall off and break something – or worse.'

'So how would Willow ride one without being seen?' Libby asked him.

'At night time it's not so much of a problem,' Reg said, 'but during the day "discretion" and "common sense" are the key words. As with every area of magic, never do anything to attract unwanted attention to yourself. Failing that, there is always an invisibility potion to consider. Some of the ingredients for that are *very* pricey.'

'Invisibility potion?' Libby said excitedly.

Ava and Willow exchanged excited looks as well.

'Magic just keeps getting cooler and cooler,' Willow said.

'Bear in mind the pricey ingredients though,' Reg was keen to point out again.

Willow went to the cheapest broomstick and ran her fingers wistfully along its wooden shaft. 'I'll take it,' she said.

Reg unclipped it from the wall and handed it to her.

The chime announced the arrival of another customer.

'Right-o, better go and see who that is,' Reg said, shuffling off. 'I'll leave you to your browsing.'

After he'd gone, Libby said, 'I was tempted to show him my wand so I could ask if it's a good quality one.'

'Why didn't you?' Ava said.

'Because I don't want to answer any awkward questions about where I got it from,' Willow responded.

'Ah, yeah,' Libby said. 'And he does seem like the type that would ask. My guess is that it's a good one. It certainly *looks* the biz. And I can't see Miss Becker having anything less than a top-notch one, can you?'

'No,' Willow agreed. Her eyes sparkled as she changed the subject: 'Hey, I wonder if you can take passengers on that broomstick.'

'Let's just see if Willow can ride it okay on her own first before we even entertain the idea of anything else,' Ava said.

'Okay,' Libby said, 'are we done in here? If that's the only one we can afford, I'm guessing that we are.'

'Shall we have another quick browse around the rest of the shop to see what else there is?' Ava said. 'And then get on our way?'

Willow and Libby agreed to this, so they all made their way back into the front area.

As they were browsing along the shelves, Ava couldn't help taking an interest in the customer that Reg was dealing with. The lady was tall and elegantly dressed, wearing a dark, wide-brimmed hat. This was positioned low over her brow, so Ava couldn't see her face well. But even so, there was something familiar about the woman. Ava was sure that she'd seen her somewhere before, but she just couldn't put her finger on when and where.

'I wonder what you'd use these for?' Libby said, scooping up a handful of blue crystals. 'It says that they're Amerite Gems.'

'I have no idea,' Willow said. 'But we know a man who will know.'

Ava tried to get a better look at the woman as she was leaving, but it was no good. The woman kept her head low and avoided eye contact with anyone.

'Shall we pay now?' Willow said. 'I'm eager to get browsing through this book.'

Libby said under her breath, 'You're eager to do something else as well.'

'Let's just pay,' Ava said, producing her money from her pocket.

Reg greeted them from behind the counter. 'Ah, you're ready, I take it?'

'We certainly are,' Libby said.

'I'm sure I don't need to tell you to be careful and discreet with your purchases,' Reg said as he took the payment, put the book in a plain paper bag and handed it to Willow, 'but I feel the need to do it anyway.' He focused his attention on Willow. 'So how did you find out that you're a witch?'

Reg's expression darkened as she explained all about the Shadowbound and everything that'd happened with regard to it.

'Well, you certainly did the right thing getting rid of *that* book,' Reg said, looking very concerned.

'We wouldn't have been able to get it away from Willow if she hadn't got her hands on another magic book,' Ava said. 'One full of good spells, rather than evil ones.'

Willow produced it from her bag and showed it to Reg.

'Ah, yes, that's a good one,' he said, nodding approval. 'I've got some of those in stock. The next obvious question is where you got it from? I'm guessing that someone gave you that book so you could wean yourself away from the other one, yes?'

Willow nodded as she tucked the book safely back into her bag. 'That's right,' she confirmed. She did not say anything else. She looked to her friends for support, but Reg had already got the message.

'Sorry, I'm prying,' he said, 'It's none of my business – but ... an evil book like the one you had is somewhat of a rarity. A real treasure to find for ... certain people, shall we say ...'

'Evil witches and wizards,' Libby said.

'Ay, that's right,' Reg said, raising a bushy eyebrow in a

manner that suggested he still wanted to take the conversation further. 'Not the sort that you want to cross, if you get my drift.'

'That problem has already been dealt with,' Ava informed him.

'Has it now?' Reg said, even more curious than ever.

'Right, well, I guess we may as well go now,' Libby said. The chime rang out as she opened the door for the others. 'Thanks for the discount and all the help you've given us.'

'It's been my pleasure,' Reg said.

Ava and Willow smiled as they went to go through the door.

'Erm,' Reg said to Willow, 'I don't suppose I could have a quick word with you on your own, could I?'

She seemed unsure of how to answer as she looked at the old man and then her friends.

'It's okay, I don't bite,' Reg assured them with a gap-toothed smile, 'and it really will only take a moment.'

Willow stepped back inside.

'We'll be just outside if you need us,' Ava said to her.

Libby and Ava stepped back and the door closed. They moved onto the pavement but kept themselves in a position where Willow could see them.

'I'm sure she'll be fine,' Libby said, 'but what do you think he wants to talk to her about?'

Ava shrugged. 'Maybe he wants to quiz her more about the evil book. We'll find out soon enough.'

Libby unlocked the bikes and then peered in through the

window, cupping her hands against the glass to cut out the glare.

A few minutes later, Willow emerged with her purchases and the girls talked as they wheeled their bikes slowly along the pavement.

'So, come on then,' Libby said, 'what did he talk to you about?'

'He's worried about you pair,' Willow said.

'Worried about us?' Ava said. 'Why?' And then she got it. 'It's because we're not magical, isn't it? He thinks that you've made a mistake by telling us – and that you should wipe our memories, just to be on the safe side.'

'That's exactly what he said,' Willow confirmed.

'And what did you say?' Libby probed.

'The same as I told Miss Becker. That you could be trusted and that memory wiping would not be needed. He pressed me on the issue, but I told him that he was wasting his time trying to convince me. He did *not* look happy with my decision. I promised him that I wouldn't tell anyone else. And that was that.'

'Did you talk about anything else?' Ava asked her.

'Just the Shadowbound,' Willow said. 'I told him which shop we'd taken it to. He said that he'd make sure that no one else got their hands on it.'

'What's he going to do with it?' Libby said.

'He isn't sure,' Willow said. 'He's going to ask some of his magical friends for their advice and take it from there.' She stopped walking and looked at the other two. 'Hey, what if he's an evil wizard and I've just told him where he can get his hands on a book that'll make him ridiculously powerful?'

'Well, number one,' Libby said, 'he came across as a pleasant old man. And, number two, the guy can hardly move, so he isn't going to be much of a threat to anybody: even with an evil book of spells.' She propped her bike against a wall and then pretended to be Reg by screwing up her face and shuffling toward Willow. 'Ay, give me that book,' she said, mimicking him. 'I know just what to do with *that*!'

Willow and Ava giggled.

'The likeness between you and him is uncanny,' Ava said, 'but, seriously, I don't think we've got anything to worry about where he's concerned.'

'You're probably right,' Willow agreed. 'But him being pleasant and not being able to move well doesn't mean that he can't be an evil wizard. That could just be an act, something to make people believe that he isn't a threat. I think you're forgetting what can be done where magic is concerned.'

'We're just going to have to take a chance on him,' Libby said.

'We took a chance on Miss Becker and look how that worked out,' Ava reminded her.

Libby said, 'Yeah, but we already knew that Miss Becker was a nasty piece of work before we even found out that she was a witch ...'

'Okay, look, can we just shut up about evil wizards and witches,' Willow said, interrupting her. 'We need to decide on where I'm going to try this thing out,' she added, holding up her broomstick. 'There's no way I'm not having a go on this thing today!'

'Remember what Reg told you about discretion,' Ava said. 'So it'll need to be somewhere you won't be seen.'

The girls mulled things over ... then Libby blurted: 'I know the perfect place. In the woods next to the school. That clearing where we've sat on that fallen tree a few times when we want to just get away from everyone. We'd still need to keep an eye out for people, but that's about as good as it's going to get without risking things too much. Whaddaya think?'

'Sounds good to me,' Willow said.

'And me,' Ava said.

The girls set off ...

34.

It didn't take them long to get there, the excitement of a broom ride pushing them to peddle frantically. Willow ignored the stares from people who were no doubt wondering why she had an old-fashioned broomstick across her handlebars. Not that she cared. She was way too pumped to give a damn.

Wheeling their bikes along the main dirt track through the woods was easy enough. It was when they broke off through a gap in the trees that the problems began. Ava, who was leading the way, got her front wheel snagged in some bushes. Libby got hit in the face by a branch. And then Willow tripped over a rock and went sprawling.

'Let's just lock the bikes up here,' Libby suggested as she helped her back to her feet.

'There's nothing to lock them to,' Willow said.

'Just lock them together,' Libby said. 'They'll be fine here.'

With that done, they set off again and it didn't take them long to find the clearing with the fallen tree.

'Right,' Willow said as she put her bag down on the trunk. She stepped into the middle of the area with the broomstick. 'O ... kay, so I have no idea what I'm supposed to do with this.'

'Try mounting it for starters,' Libby said.

'Oh, well, I couldn't have guessed that I'd have needed to do that,' Willow replied, sliding it between her legs. 'Got any more tips?' she said with a smile.

'Try imagining yourself taking off,' Ava suggested. 'See if that works.'

Willow did just that – and stayed rooted to the spot.

'Perhaps Reg has sold you a duff one?' Libby said, amused. 'It's probably just a normal broomstick that's only good for sweeping the floor.'

Willow scowled. 'How am I supposed to focus if you're acting the goat?'

'Sorry,' Libby said, struggling not to smile as she ran her fingers across her lips in a zipping gesture. 'Not another word until you're airborne. I promise.'

'Try and concentrate again,' Ava said to Willow, 'but give it longer this time.'

Willow nodded. She closed her eyes for a second and then opened them, looking fully focused. And ... nothing happened. She remained rooted to the spot, her shoes half immersed in fallen leaves.

Ava was tempted to say something, but she bit down on her lip instead – then watched in amazement as Willow rose slowly into the air and began hovering a few feet above the ground.

'Woo-hoo! *Yeah!*' Libby screeched, prancing on her toes excitedly. 'You did it!'

'Cool!' Ava said, clapping. 'And now for what could be the more difficult bit. Can you fly around on it?'

Willow leaned forward slightly and flew toward the other two. They moved out of the way just in time and watched as she shot past them.

'Careful you don't fly into a tree or something!' Ava warned her.

'It's surprisingly easy to control.' Willow said as she now began looping around above them, 'I want to go higher! I want to soar up to the clouds!'

'*NO!*' Ava said as she watched her continue to loop. 'Remember what Reg told you!'

'I want to know if that thing can carry more than one person,' Libby said.

Willow swooped down beside her and beckoned her to get on.

Libby did not need prompting twice. She slid on behind

her friend and put her hands around her waist.

'Hold on tight!' Willow advised her.

Libby screeched 'I *willllllllllllll!*' as they shot upward and began looping overhead. 'Now this is what I call fun!' she called down to Ava. 'You've got to have a go at this! You've just got to!'

And she did. When Willow landed again, Ava took Libby's position and up in the air once again went the broomstick.

Ava savored every moment of her time whizzing around with the wind in her face, stinging her eyes. *Magic can't get any cooler than this*, she thought. *Nothing can be cooler than this!* But then she imagined what it would be like to fly over mountains and lakes and cities and knew that it could ...

35.

All three girls were buzzing as they walked their bikes back out along the path. The sky above had darkened with the promise of rain, so they were hurrying to get home before the inevitable happened.

'So where am I supposed to hide this?' Willow said, nodded toward the broomstick, which she'd laid back over her handlebars. 'And if my parents find it, what possible excuse can I come up with for having it?'

Ava said, 'Just tell them that someone had put it out to be chucked away and that you've always wanted a broomstick that looks like the sort a witch would own.'

'My mum will moan about it cluttering up the house,'

Willow said, 'and my dad will probably try and sweep the floor with it.'

'There must be somewhere you can hide it,' Libby said. 'And what about a magical solution? Is there a spell for making things small? *That* would solve the problem.'

'I'm sure I noticed something like that in the book,' Willow said. 'I'll have a look through when I get home (until then, I'll just have to stash it somewhere). Hey, speaking of home, would you pair like to come to my house tomorrow? My parents will be gone for most of the day, visiting their friends, so I'll have the place to myself. We can have a really good look through my books. Who knows, maybe we can cobble enough ingredients together for a basic potion.'

'I'm in,' Libby said.

'It'll have to be after twelve,' Ava said, 'because we've got that detention, remember?'

'Oh yeah! I'd forgotten about that!' Libby said. 'Our hour of fun with Amy and Bogey Girl. What a riot of laughs that's going to be. I wonder what we'll be doing. Mrs Fernsby will probably have us checking under all the desks to see if any bogies need cleaning off.'

Willow retched. 'Ahhh, no – that is *gross!* But I must admit that I'll be checking the underside of any desk I sit at in school from now on.'

The girls continued to talk as they walked with their bikes. They arranged to meet the following day at Willow's house at 1 pm so that they could spend some time exploring the boundaries of what could and could not be done with magic.

A steady drizzle began to fall as they reached the main road. A few minutes later this became a torrential downpour. Needless to say, the girls got drenched as they rode their bikes home. And they laughed their heads off all the way ...

36.

In the morning, at eight on the dot, Mrs Greenwood woke Ava and told her that the detention had been cancelled. At first, this had seemed like good news – but then Mrs Greenwood informed her that it would be rescheduled for the following Saturday or the one after that.

'Did she give a reason?' Ava asked as she stretched beneath her covers.

'She gave two. First was that one of the girls would be a no-show and the second was because of some urgent personal business that needs to be sorted. Funny, I thought you'd be happier than this. And yet here you are, still looking half asleep, and almost nonplussed.'

'I would have preferred to just get it over and done with, to be honest.'

Ava didn't need two guesses as to who the no-show would be.

'Yes, well,' Mrs Greenwood said, 'sometimes in life there are things that impact you that you have no influence over. This is a prime example. All you can do is roll with it and get on with other things ... things that you *can* influence.'

'What, like a nice lie-in?' Ava said, managing a cheeky

smile. 'Can I have some influence over that? Another thirty minutes would be nice.'

The look on Mrs Greenwood's face suggested not – but then her expression softened and she nodded. 'Fine. Don't go wasting all morning in bed, though. I can find plenty of things for you to do that are a lot more productive than a lie-in.'

I bet you can, Ava thought as she watched her leave the room.

Staring up at the ceiling with her eyes half-open, Ava tried to nod back off but just couldn't. The conversation with her mother had fired her brain cells into action. As a result, all she could do now was think about what she was going to do for the rest of the morning. She had five hours to kill.

Her thoughts were blank for a moment. And then she recalled the trip to The Mystic Magic the previous day. What fun that'd been! She'd loved every second of it: the anticipation during the cycle ride there; the excitement and mystery of browsing shelves full of magical items. And, of course, there was the potions book to consider. Ava couldn't wait to see what sort of concoctions could be created. In her mind, she played out everything that'd happened in the shop – from the moment the door chime had announced their arrival right up to the point where Reg had quizzed them about the Shadowbound.

According to Willow, Reg had said that he would make sure no one else got their hands on it. The more Ava thought about this, the more it alarmed her. Had Willow made a mistake by telling him where he could obtain the book? He had come across as being a nice person. But, as Willow had pointed out before, this did not necessarily mean that he wasn't an evil wizard. Her instincts told her that he probably wasn't. Her instincts were, however, also telling her that it was sometimes wise to assume the worst.

This got her moving. She sprang out of bed and got herself dressed: pulling on a pair of bottoms, a T-shirt and a thick black jumper. When Ava told her parents that she was nipping out, they asked the inevitable question: where to?

Ava saw no reason to lie. 'To the bookshop in Harwich,' she responded proudly. 'I've only been in there once and I'd like to look around again. I've still got birthday money to spend.'

'Money spent on books will never be money wasted,' Mr Greenwood said with an approving nod.

Ava noted the time on her way out. She wanted to make sure she was first through the door and had twenty-five minutes to get there (assuming a normal opening time of 9 am); so off she set on her bike, whizzing along with the wind in her face. She felt nervous about the task ahead, but also quite exhilarated and excited. She pedaled as fast as she could, as though she were racing against an invisible person. She leaned into corners so she could take them quickly. She kept her body low and compact so she could be as streamlined as possible on the straights. And she arrived dead at 9 am, just in time to see a man flip the sign on the door from **CLOSED** to **OPEN**. Fortunately, he didn't notice

Ava as he was doing this. She moved back out of sight as he was jiggling the key in the lock.

Ava wheeled her bike down the street so she could secure it to the nearest lamppost. It was as she was uncurling the lock from beneath her seat that she heard the door open and the bell announce someone's arrival. She turned just in time to catch a glimpse of that someone entering the shop. *So much for being first*, Ava thought dismally.

She quickly finished securing the bike and into the shop she went, the bell announcing her arrival. Unlike The Book Cove, this shop was on one level: a huge expanse of an area, lined with aisles full of tall bookshelves.

Ava looked left to see if anyone was behind the counter, but there was no one to be seen. There was no sign of the person who'd entered before her, either. Ava had no idea where the magic book section was, but all the books around her were fiction so she began making her way down the nearest aisle.

She heard voices as she got closer to the back of the room, where the non-fiction books were displayed. They grew louder as she got closer to the far corner. Cautiously stepping into this area, Ava moved down an aisle to the far left, a safe distance away from the voices — but close enough to overhear what was being said:

'How did you come by this book?' a woman said.

Ava recognized the voice but couldn't put a face to it.

'It was brought in yesterday by a young girl,' came a reply from what Ava assumed to be the shopkeeper. 'She told me that she didn't need it anymore. Looks like it could be an ... interesting read.'

'Oh yes,' the woman replied, 'it's going to be a *very* interesting read, all right.'

Ava continued to puzzle over the woman's voice and where she'd heard it before. But it was only when she heard a third voice join the conversation that the penny dropped.

'Please tell me that we're now going to look at some books that are more interesting than some fake collection of magic spells? I mean, why are you even bothering with it, Mum? Wouldn't you be better off with one about cookery or something?'

Ruth! No! Ava thought, realizing what this could mean. She remembered back to the Mystic Magic and the mysterious woman who'd entered the shop. Then she remembered where she'd seen the woman before that: at a parents' evening about a month before. Totally in shock, Ava continued to listen.

'As if I have time for things like cooking,' Mrs Ribble said as if such a thing was way beneath her.

'Right, I'm going to have to leave you to your browsing as I have some new stock to sort through,' the shopkeeper said. 'If you need any help with anything, just give me a holler and I'll find you.'

'Thank you for your time,' Mrs Ribble said.

Ava peeked around the bookcase just in time to see the shopkeeper heading for the middle aisle.

'We just need to sort you out with some books and then

we'll be done,' Mrs Ribble said to Ruth.

'Why do I even have to read books anyway?' she protested. 'They're so boring!'

'And what about your detention this morning?' Mrs Ribble said. 'Would that have been any more or less boring? Just be thankful that I've gotten you out of that and that I'm not confining you to your bedroom with nothing to do but stare out of the window.'

'Mrs Fernsby will rearrange the detention for another weekend,' Ruth said, 'so you haven't gotten me out of anything. All you've done is delay it.'

Both of them had moved to the right, so Ava now had a good view of them.

Mrs Ribble was once again elegantly attired: this time in a long floral dress and high-heeled shoes, which made clip-clopping sounds on the wooden floor as she walked. Ruth was the complete opposite in terms of style: sporting scuffed jeans and a light blue top. Ava wouldn't have put them together if she didn't know that they were related.

Mrs Ribble had the Shadowbound clutched tightly to her chest as if it were something she'd been looking for her whole life and finally found. Ava thought that this could well have been the case.

Mrs Ribble loomed over her daughter. 'I have an appointment with Mrs Fernsby on Monday after school,' she said, caressing the book with her fingers. 'We're going to sit down and have a good chat about things, me and your headmistress. She's had it in for you ever since you started at that school. Or, at least, that's the way it feels to me. And I'm not going to stand for it any longer. That woman will bend to my will, whether she likes it or not. Life at school for you will be a lot easier after that. And then you will have no excuses for underperforming. Let's be clear about that.'

Ruth looked as if she wanted to say something – but she kept her mouth shut.

A rare, smart move from you, Ava thought. She wondered if Ruth had told her mother about the bogie incident. *I'm going to guess that you haven't.*

'You scurry ahead and check out the fiction section,' Mrs Ribble said, shooing her daughter away with quick flicks of her long, wiry fingers, 'and I'll be along in a minute.'

Ruth didn't need prompting twice. She moved toward the front of the shop.

After she'd gone, Mrs Ribble looked at the book and smiled. 'Oh, what a sweet, sweet find you are,' she said, turning the pages without having to touch them. Her eyes were wide with excitement as she took in the text. 'I can already feel the power coursing through me.' She stood there for about another minute, transfixed by the book.

Until Ruth called out to her: 'Mum, are you coming? I've found three already!'

Mrs Ribble tutted in annoyance, then replied: 'Yes! I'll be there in a minute!' In a lower voice, she added: 'Honestly, girl, if only you knew what you're capable of – but you are not quite ready for *that* revelation yet.'

Ava watched, dumbfounded, as Mrs Ribble went to join

her daughter. After Ava had lost sight of her, she fell back against the bookcase she'd been hiding behind and slid down it. Her backside hit the floor with a thump. She stared at the wall but saw nothing. Her body felt numbed by what she'd just heard. *No!* she thought. *Not her! Of all people, not her!* Finding out that Ruth's mother was a witch had been bad enough. That'd been awful news – but this was even *worse*. Ava continued to stare at the wall, lost in her thoughts.

Five minutes later, she heard the doorbell ring out, announcing that someone had either entered or left the shop. She hoped that it was the latter as she gave it a few more minutes then headed for the door.

Just as she was about to leave, the shopkeeper called out to her from behind the counter, 'Err, excuse me! ...'

But that was all that Ava heard as she ignored him and exited the shop. She checked left and right but couldn't see Ruth or her mother anywhere, which was good. Quickly unlocking her bike, Ava set off down the road, peddling as fast as she could, her knees a blur of speed. She needed to let her friends know that there was a storm coming – and that the girl who'd been their nemesis was going to be at the center of it ...

Dear readers, as you've probably guessed, this is not the end of the story. Why end here? Two reasons, really: one, the book would have ended up too long and the printing costs would have been prohibitive; two, after such a big revelation, I thought that this would be a good place to pause for setting up the next book. If you do decide to leave a review, please bear in mind that this is just the first instalment and that there's a lot more to come. I hope you enjoyed reading this as much as I enjoyed writing it.

Follow CJ Loughty on Facebook for news and updates:
https://tinyurl.com/wudx96za

Printed in Great Britain
by Amazon